Under the Sink

Selected Works

by d.a. peters

Published by D.A. Peters Press

Parts of this text resembling persons, places, and events are
purely coincidental.

Written, copyedited, cover design, and interior photography by
d.a. peters

Printed and bound in the U.S. by:

Lulu Enterprises, Inc.
3101 Hillsborough St
Raleigh, NC 27607-5436

ISBN 978-0-578-03611-3

Contents

I. <u>Author's Preface</u>

If you're reading this, it means I finally finished writing.

I'd like to thank the academy.

I started writing this collection back in fall of 2004, while attending Brigham Young University, an evangelical Mormon school in Utah. I was barely 18. The novella featured here was more or less a journal of my thoughts from the summer and the one prior.

Our professor, Nathan Chai, had given us the advice that we should "make the familiar seem new; the new seem familiar." So, I wrote what I knew (at 18, it was cleaning toilets, pushing carts, and cooking Chinese food). I was also going through a crisis at the time.

I didn't want to be a part of the Mormon Church and couldn't figure a way out without disappointing family, except running away. Scotland came to mind but it could've been anywhere. Somehow, that made more sense than just coming out and accepting that being yourself has consequences – especially from those around you. I had to learn to deal with it.

Of course, I didn't learn that till years later. Instead, I spent nearly nine-hundred dollars on airplane tickets to Heathrow Airport. This is all true. The only thing that prevented me from running was a visa.

I forgot that step in my planning.

So, I faced the music and realized I had to do my homework if I wasn't going to run away with some buxom Scottish woman.

Parts of the following stories came from these decisions and the "what-if" of going through with such an audacious plan.

Oh, and I was struggling with puberty like every other adolescent male, hence the airplane scene. You'll know it when you see it.

The writing came easy but I had no direction, nowhere to lead all these characters, these everyday people with problems a little larger than themselves.

It took coming out to my family, joining the Marine Corps, and dropping out of that wonderful (no, really!) university of mine.

The detour took a little over four years and I'd be arrogant (and foolish not) to say that it spanned three continents. I've gone clubbing in central Europe. I've watched the sunset on the beaches of Iwo Jima. I've known the love of a few good women despite being as decisive and sure of my direction as a boy scout with a broken compass.

There are a few people I wish to thank:

1) My professor, Nathan Chai, who encouraged me to pick up authors like Darrell Spencer, John Updike, and Chuck Palahniuk. It helped me find my own voice writing.

2) Marine Corps. Oorah, Semper Fidelis, and thanks for putting up with me. It wasn't easy but stuff that's worth anything never is. Webster, Blair, Azzone, Stanley, Millhouse, Smith, and Ottoman: you kept me sane.

3) My family. They've supported me in nearly every capacity over the years. I've been a handful (from infancy) but I just wanted to say I love them.

And finally, for aspiring authors, remember this:

When life gives you shit, start planting.

-d.a. peters

January 26, 2009

History by Numbers
(a novella)

II.   Under the Sink: Chris' Story

Fiona broke up with me last Thursday. I remember -not because of how I took all the photos I had of her and made a creamy, pulp smoothie for my greyhound, Gen- but because of the five o'clock rush at work that day. If no one's told you, I'm a cook.

No, I was a straight "A" student in high school.

No, it wasn't because of my Chinese heritage.

Yes, my parents were strict in my studies - when they were there.

My father wanted me to be a doctor or a lawyer, lots of good money there. My mother wanted me to teach college. I-

-I grew up cooking in our family's pan-Asian buffet. When I say Asian, I mean the food that Americans associate with the Orient - General Tso, Sweet and Sour, Orange Glaze Chicken. Lots of chicken and a side of broccoli beef all of it covered in the dollar brand tempura batter. I used woks, steamers, even the flat hibachi grill.

That's what I knew and -in lack of direction after four years of high school- it was easy to fall back on. Now, it's three years on.

Of course, I never told my parents. They think I'm a student in Bellingham, Washington - chasing the women while maintaining a 3.9 average. My father says I'll do better next year.

That day, I remember cooking some thirty pounds of product. That lasted under an hour. You lose about that much to shrinkage on a really slow night after a mid-afternoon rush. You make too much and no one shows; you put too much in and get

7

nothing in return. Twenty pounds is the average we'd toss a night.

People really went for Empress Chicken, an oyster-sauce flavor I could never get into. I preferred spice - a little burn that stuck with you than a sweet that'd get forgotten with yesterday's news.

They say you lose your sense of taste after cooking so often.

It's a lie from what my mouth tells me.

You just lose your love for a particular flavor - you can still taste it all you want.

It's not unlike life.

Fiona sneezes after orgasm - every time.

I met her at a party, long before she started work at Glouster's. I was nervous and she came up to me, my hand trembling as the plastic cup dribbles onto my tongue. She said she found my Parkinson's attractive.

I don't have Parkinson's - my grandfathers did.

I remember thinking "what a douche thing to say to a stranger."

I mean the set-up went:

[Insert joke about a terminal disease subject has]

[Wait for laughter]

[Get drink poured on head]

I didn't do that though. I don't exactly hit things off with the ladies - not ever. Instead, Mr. Popularity here shut up worse than an agoraphobic mollusk. I just want away from here: from this town and from this land.

In my youth, my father presented me with a pocket watch his grandfather found in Hong Kong. The story goes that the watch belonged to a U.S. Marine during the years of the Boxer Rebellion. It still functioned and my father kept it well polished on the mantel in his office at work. Every day -at noon- he'd reset it.

When I turned eight, he gave it to me on the Southport Spit along the Gold Coast. The waves crashed on the beach, breaking over the shoals and sandbars.

I put in my pocket, returning to my sand castles and splashing in the waves.. It'd be years later that that he told me the meaning:

He was walking in the British section of Hong Kong during 1979 when he went to check his pocket watch. It was frozen. He stopped to ask a small, pretty woman for the time. It was my mother. She talked with him for thirty minutes after helping adjust his watch. She'd been an immigrant from Cambodia, a refugee from the Khmer Rouge. All the shit people talk about China they really fail to realize we were better off than many. The prospect of marrying a respectable, charming young man when your extended family was rotting in prison for dissent (read: teaching English values and trading with foreigners) is good enough for anyone.

My father's parents met hers -also escaped the regime- and an arrangement was made. In 1980, they filed for marriage in a government courthouse. They left in 1983 during a lax period in Australia's immigration policy, sneaking aboard a cargo ship with a satchel of food for the entire journey. Fortunately, they fit in well enough with my mother's English language background.

I suppose stories like that sound cliché but every now and again, they happen. They have to, right?

Fiona wound up working at Glouster's last year and we eventually dated. It's a small, rural town: I must've seemed exotic to her. Americans and their love for Asian import models.

I can say this, having been born overseas. Our family moved during the mid-nineties from Sydney to San Francisco. I was ten at the time and just discovered music my parents could hate: Nine Inch Nails and Public Enemy. Both clung to abrasion and -yet- mellowed to some beautiful melodies.

Fiona came over as I was flipping the contents of the wok over the flames.

"Got some chicken, chicken?"

To be fair - I didn't date her based on sense of humor. It was one of those one sided relationships where I'm not particularly funny but she was exceptionally so.

It worked though. I didn't need a comedienne. I just needed someone who encouraged me to do anything with pigeonholing me into professions with eight years of schooling. Bill Gates dropped out of college; look at how happy he is. Same thing with Steve Jobs. He claimed to come up with the font you're reading this in because of a calligraphy class he dropped out of.

Sometimes failing college is the best way to learn how not to study in the future. We all need subversion, some excuse to get out below the all-seeing dollar sign. People are happy as butchers, chefs, computer programmers with mere certificates: college is mere one of many things people can do to feel accomplished. If you want to feel good, college is just an option.

Michael, the deli and Asian Express customer clerk sits on the side of the building, back against the burnt-orange brick. He's a little older. We're sharing a cigarette -one of many lasts-.

"How long have Fiona and you been in love?"

I laugh a little.

"We're not in love in that storybook way, man. We just live together and been dating for a while now."

"Is it serious?"

I turn to him and raise my eyebrow, "there something you should be telling me, like you're gay and secretly want my body?"

"No. You two just seemed kind of distant when together."

I nod and put down my cigarette, stamping it in the grass.

Fiona had this terrible Catholic sense of guilt, even though she attended an Anglican service since the age of sixteen. She wouldn't want to be seen naked after sex and promptly dressed – much like when never cross paths with a black cat or never drove anything smaller than a Sport-Utility Vehicle..

"I don't see why god is so concerned with your naughty bits."

"I - I just don't want you to view me as cheap."

"I get your argument but I don't see why we can't just rest here a bit."

"Oh, you want to cuddle - fag."

I throw a pillow at her. She chortles, obviously congested by the barely tepid Puget Sound fall. My ass completely bare now, I pull the blankets up around my neck.

"I don't get it though."

"My argument?"

"No, god - I don't get god."

'You never get god - you'll never get him until you pray."

"I just don't see the point of jumping into the dark."

As a child in Australia, I once saw a koala caught in a dingo trap. I was playing with a dilapidated Qantas plane my father bought for me in the city. The koala squirmed and struggled to get free, thrashing in ways they never seem to do. They're normally such deliberate animals, walking like children taking first steps but without the teetering and the falling.

Her leg is torn and bleeding. Tufts of fur stick out from under the teeth and bits of flesh already dry to the rusted metal.

As a child, you think everyone needs help. You can't accept that the world falls apart yet. My blue shorts sat belly-button high as I grabbed a rail spike and went over to her, careful where I stepped and hunched over.

I reach out and-

-it bites me, hard. It clamps down and won't let go. All I remember is rage and pain as I hit it over the head with the spike.

It eventually let go but not without a small chunk missing.

The way it lashed out when it was pained - lashed out at those helping. It stuck with me.

"But you said I could get Friday off?"

"No can do."

"You scheduled it."

"Well, James called in sick and we've already borrowed enough staff from the Mount Vernon branch, so you're it."

"Alright."

I go back to stirring the honey garlic sauce till it bubbles.

What's the point of life if all you get is lied to? What drives you when all you do is get driven over, time and time again?

I just want out of here.

Don't get me wrong, I love small towns. I'd love to relocate someday: someplace different. I have the money saved up. I have no social life aside from Fiona and World of Warcraft.

Fiona's underage and under-the-influence after five P.M. on Fridays. It's a routine for her. She'll crack open six pack of Smirnoff ICE and down it like a champ. Definitely wouldn't make a good nurse.

Ever since she stopped attending youth group (at eighteen no less), she's pounded the bottle, iterant as ever.

"Are you going to be home tonight?"

"No, I'm pulling a late shift - quarterly inventory of all the food: bamboos shoots to the zucchini"

"I'm going to bed early then. I love you."

"Well, take care."

In retrospect, I never said "I love you" back - ever.

The day we broke up, she told me she was going to her Grandma's in Coquitlam. I wished her well.

I got a special evening planned for her return: washed my hatchback, got scented candles for the table, and even ironed my flannel shirt. Yes, an Asian in flannel. Go, ahead, laugh at me.

I was in some kind of love -or something like it.

You know the type that keeps your fingernails clean.

I go into work, excited for once, and see her arguing with department manager.

"You can't just get drunk every night and expect nothing to happen at work, you work with slicers and deep-fryers. You can't work drunk. It's against company policy. I mean, Jesus, crossed the border and saw no repercussions? "

"Screw company policy. I do a damn good job. Everyone here loves me; they say I do a great job."

"No, they don't."

"What?"

"Your peers say you always need help, you're a little slow training and you let the older women do most of the work.

She looks off at him in defeat.

"Fuck that, I'm doing good."

"No, you don't - watch your language."

"Or what?"

"Can we speak privately?"

"No, you tell it to my face."

He paused, calmly.

"You're fired."

When I asked what happened, she told me everything was fine. She said she'd just been at her Grandma's.

When I confronted her, she denied it. She denied and denied until she broke down in tears in my arms.

She asked if I'd forgive her.

I wanted to cry, wanted to lash out, wanted… something but I just rub my right hand in pain. She asked if it was because she hurt me.

"No, I said. Lying to me doesn't hurt; never being able to trust you again - that does."

That day I hated the sight of raw chicken in panko crumbs. I hated the slimy feel of the fat before you fry it. I hated the smell of the Sambal Olek Chili sauce.

There's stench in the sink after washing a day's worth of chicken meat – you just block it out. It was an irony though. Removing me from the scene is what helped me as a cook.

If you try too hard, you lose that knack for instinct.

Like you know what crackling sound means the tempura is just crisp enough or what color the beef strips should be before caramelizing in the teriyaki sauce.

I could've worked at a Teppanyaki restaurant, not the fast food section of a grocery store-

-but this is what I loved, right? I hated offices but saw no future outdoors. The great thing about line cooking is no one cares. One of our cooks kept his cigar tucked in his sleeve for breaks; another cursed and listened to the Ramones.

I mean, I only did this because I didn't fit in anywhere else.

The roads are slick and icy as I ride my bike home. I'm furious and disappointed. I couldn't care less there's a patch up ahead or that I'll skid into an intersection and get hit by a car pulling out on a green light.

I don't care, even after I roll across the windshield.

The driver gets out,

"My god, ARE YOU OKAY?"

She shouts like I just go off the boat."

"Yes, ma'am. I didn't feel a thing."

It's a stranger; strangers are fair game to lie to.

"Well, you're bleeding."

"Of course I am. That's life."

I pick up my satchel and a tuft of hair falls to the ground, no clue where it's from.

My front tire is bent and lopsided.

15

I wheel the bike back to my apartment to find a note tapped to my doorbell.

"Chris,

"There's so much I can't share about me. So much of my life that you'll never know - or maybe you should. I dot' know.

"I was glad of the time we spent together and hope you can forgive me.

"xo,

"Fiona"

I'm a sentimental guy; I keep every letter my parents write, every birthday card from grandparents. I'm a good son like that.

I purchased a shredder from OfficeMax the day I got that letter.

I lost my verbal warning at work early on when I took two jobs to pay for the community college. I dropped out.

"What are you going to do about it?"

At this point, I'm done with a lot of things. I don't want to cook, don't want to be reminded of this place.

"What I'm going to do? I'm probably going to go masturbate in the men's room and forget about it."

"What? That last comment was uncalled for."

"Look, I'm just under a lot of stress right now."

"You need to turn in your badge."

"Fine by me, I need a change of scenery."

I walk away and then stop to turn:

"And one more thing: you'll never guess how I put the jerk in Jerk Chicken. Bon appétit!"

There goes the last tie I'll ever wear.

Give me a chance and I'll disappear on the road. Give me a compass and I'll lose it. In the Bay Area, I'd go running - directionless. I'd just set out in a direction, taking turns as I pleased. It didn't matter: the Castro, Chinatown, Civic Center, Oceanview.

My senior year, I grabbed two of my best friends and two girls, filling my five seater. We went to Vegas on a Wednesday afternoon - a school day in March.

We walked the strip, my first time in the city. Caesar's Palace and the nude classical statues were sodomized by the girls. A toothless hooker crossed the skyway. It smelled of urine. We gambled my car's coin tray. All in all, a very productive night of studying.

We made it back by the last period of Thursday. My mother cursed me out for skipping school but my father couldn't stop laughing.

I'm packing my stuff like a drug dealer: three tees, two long sleeve, three sets jeans, two pairs shoes, five pairs socks, no briefs. I don't care what else I pack. I have my money ready, in cash, supposedly for college. Supposedly, I'm sane too. I drained my checking account to buy tickets for Heathrow and to secure a shuttle ride at 5 a.m. to the airport. I'd have more but I bought first-class. Might as well run-away in comfort. All I have now is cash. The blood on forehead, palms, wrists, and feet flakes off.

I grab the phone, "Michael? You alright?"

"Yes.

"Listen, your family was looking for a dog? I'll give you my greyhound if you promise to take care of her."

There's an elderly gentleman next to me. He's the kind that thinks he's "oh-so" funny. The kind who belches loudly then laughs at you. The kind who watches Sesame Street with the sound off, pant-less. One of those types: he's sitting next to me.

"What's your name, young man?"

The smell of pine trees, beer, and a dozen intangibles gnaw at my nostrils.

"Did you run away from home?"

How old does he think I am?

"It's okay, I like you."

He's trying so hard to say his words. They slur on occasion, but he's trying not to.

"Do you like candy?" he chortles.

I shake my head. I want to get off.

"Just reach into my pocket and I have a surprise for you."

I jump back, only to run toward the exit. I'll walk the last three miles to Seatac International.

A sign reads, "Buckle up. Listen to your elders."

The walk is cold. Everything seems dampened: sounds, lights, and especially touch. I take out my sweater to keep warm. The environment won't affect me.

I can't get the image of that man out of my mind. I feel sorry for him. That's what I'm supposed to do. Pity the wayward soul no matter how lost. In a way, I do. Then I remember him placing my hand on his thigh.

I shiver.

A sign reads, "Respect your elders."

I stumble, aimlessly shifting around the airport. Weather delays are the only reason I'll make my flight. The tickets are non-refundable, so I'd be out eight-hundred dollars. I only have the same amount in my pocket, for living expense. There's something about the usual carousel of shops at an airport: the duty free store with overpriced chocolate and liquor, the beer garden with imported lager, the half dozen Starbuck's within the square mile. I see the flower shop, with its Valentine's Day line of cards.

Inside, my first thought is that love is an airport. No excess baggage. No refunds. Expect delays. No pets onboard. Mid-air collisions. You know that warm fuzzy feeling when you meet someone: that's third degree burns over 90% of your body.

Hell, the last girl I dated had frequent flier miles.

To me: love was stored in the overhead.

The plane arrives and I sit down as other passengers begin to board: a band, a family, and a couple. They're all smiles and laughs and looking forward. They're genuinely happy and in love. I hope the Grim Reaper slips Cupid some roofies next time they meet.

I yawn and try reclining; the seat won't move.

"This is broken."

A flight attendant says, "Sir, you already have the seat back."

Nevermind. A girl boards the plane. Brown hair to the shoulder, held up by a crow hair-pin. She's wearing a plaid skirt, not the loose, school-girl type. The type you see in magazines. Her combat boots reach the knee. She walks through a puff of smoke as she extinguishes a cigarette. Her lips are red. Her baby-blue sweater folds around all the right surfaces, with a white dress-shirt poking out. Her messenger bag is light. Her legs are long. She stops next to my row, dropping a pair of glasses from her bag. Leaning over, she picks them up. This is what heaven looks like to an adolescent male.

She springs upward and rests her hands on her shoulder. She turns.

"Is this row 13?" Her accent is cute, in a don't-mess-with-me way.

"Yes."

"Can I sit here? I hate the window."

"Sure."

She sits down, looking off into the distance.

She's reading some book: memento or morrie or breakfast with morrie. Memento morrie? Something like that; something I've never heard of.

She faces me once more.

"Stop eye-humping me."

I look up and catch those eyes.

She flips me off.

Eight hundred dollars and I'm locked in the upright position.

"Attention passengers, this is your captain speaking..."

The plane's delayed for three hours: something about electrical tape, tampons, and the Women's Liberation Confederacy. Whatever. I feel like those people in fabric softener commercials after my nap. I feel lithium.

"So where are you from?"

"You're awake?"

"Yeah. Why haven't we left?"

"Delays."

She scrunches her eyebrows together. A "wha…" escapes her lips.

"Don't ask."

"Could you shut the blinds?"

"Sure."

"Thanks."

"You're welcome".

She looks ahead, trying to figure out if we're going to move. No use.

"So where are you from?"

"The States."

"Really… that's a surprise." Her eyebrows rise.

"I'm from Washington. What's your name?" I extend my hand toward hers.

"Morana. I'm from Scotland."

"Where-abouts?"

"Edinburgh." A sigh escapes those burgundy lips.

"Are you familiar with Scotland?"

"Just books. My family is from Australia and before that China."

"Neat. Well, now that you know my name-"

"I'm Chris Tam."

"Christian? Really?"

"No, just Chris."

We're talking. She's laughs, occasionally covering her nose while drinking.

The plane takes off and a drink cart passes us. The attendant moves ahead, smiling and trying her best not to punch a man in business class. Morana pulls a scotch off.

"Hey... we just can't..."

She covers my mouth, and pulls vodka from the back of her skirt.

"I don't drink vodka."

"Not once?"

"Never."

She hands me the bottle.

"Cheers."

"I can't. I shouldn't."

The drink is hardly chilled any more, what with her turning the other cheek. I try not to think of it. No one would approve.

I take a swig. It burns all the way down.

She drinks from her bottle: almost the whole thing.

"Scotch going out of style?"

She snorts alcohol out her nose.

"You bet."

"Must sting."

"You're a riot, you."

Alcohol spurts out again, all over my hunter green sweater.

We laugh.

"It just might be passé."

"If Scotch is going out of style, I wonder about this sweater now."

She laughs harder.

"Come, I'll clean you off."

The alcohol is really taking its effect now. My mind is great. I don't have a care in the world, save the girl taking me by the hand.

Morana pulls me into the bathroom and slams the door. It's slightly larger in first class.

She leans close, reaching around my waist. She takes my sweater off.

"Looks like it didn't get the undershirt."

"It got yours."

She looks down.

"It did."

She begins taking off her sweater, leaving her blouse.

"It got the blouse too."

She finally notices the cut in my lip, the bruised face, and dirty hands.

"Your scabs are bleeding. How old are they?"

"A few hours."

"That long?"

"What else is new?"

"Here." She rips some toilet paper and begins soaking up the blood.

"They say alcohol prevents clotting."

"No shite."

She's close, her breath coming off her lips and onto my chin.

"This is bad."

Her nose draws closer to mine, "really?"

She moves closer, pressing herself against my battered frame. I could collapse under all of this. That would be....

"Yeah, real bad."

We kiss: lips press against each other, like rose petals. Never felt this before. So new and fresh as her face flusters pink in the light.

It's warmer now. The touch, the feel: these moments are the fabric of our lives. This is heaven, forget the above and the below. Just go on. Press forward. Endure to the end. I want it last, for a time or even the eternities.

She draws back.

"Yeah. This is bad."

She laughs and pulls hair from out of her face.

"It could be worse."

"Really?"

"Yeah. Really."

God, I really want this to last. I'm thinking this might be it: my slice of permanence for my new life.

She locks the door and lays her hands upon me.

"Now you're stuck in heaven."

Next thing you know, we're speaking in tongues.

Morana sleeps next to me. No, we'd didn't have sex. I knew you were thinking that - don't. Shame on you. We just made out in the bathroom and confessed that we'd both come out of bad relationships. Her boyfriend had cheated on her so deeply and so long that she claimed it wasn't her first time making out with a stranger.

For all my usual gripes with that concept (*since it happens so much*), I couldn't care less about how many lips have touched hers, just that mine touched hers and we could bitch about past flames in reasonable comfort.

The speakers chime.

"This is your captain speaking: we're expecting some slight turbulence."

Morana lifts her head off my thigh. It twinges from falling asleep.

"What?"

Nothing important. Just a warning.

"Um... okay. Whatever."

My mouth curls up on a side and I just shrug.

For all the turbulence, the skies at our elevation are clear. We're just about the cloud level with that blue-black of oblivion above us. Updrafts.

"Attention all passengers. Please remain calm."

They say that, fully aware the passengers were calm up until then.

"We're losing some cabin pressure and masks will drop from the ceiling. Please put them on per our hostesses' instructions."

They sitting down, already wearing masks. The black box doesn't have a video camera of the passenger cabin.

Morana gets up, arching her back with a yawn.

"We're going to make an emergency water landing."

I turn my head to her and whisper, "That's a euphemism for crash."

She turns to me, just as nonchalant, "Least I brought my floaties."

We burst into laughter nervously. The rest of the cabin is panicked and we're hooting and crowing. An older women looks at us with disdain.

"Well, my dear, if this is it. I never intended on writing you when we get to England."

"Me neither, and I doubt we'll get to England at this pace."

"At least the not-sex was good."

We start laughing again, nervous and loud.

Outside we can see the horizon get bigger; it's taking up the left side now. He's not landing so much as he's rolling the 787 over in its sleep.

"You'd think they'd go to college for something like this?"

The noise is intense outside. The whistling, the roaring: all reminders of what cold awaits and how we feel right now. Turbulence is apt.

With a large, hollow creak the plane hits the water. I was half hoping for a splash like a chubby kid in a pool. People scramble to the doors, inflating the rafts and their collars. I grip my seat handles, grabbing her hand.

Morana and I, we just sit.

"You're taking this rather calmly," she said.

"Calm? I think I peed a little."

"Really?"

"I was being sarcastic - breaking the ice for you."

"Well, I -"

"I want to tell you something, only because I like you and because it can't hurt you and me at this point."

"Oh my god, you're gay?"

I look down and laugh.

"No-"

"You're a woman?"

"No, nevermind."

She looked off at the emergency door.

"Hey, points for honesty, right?"

"Come on, let's go?" she says, taking my hand. I grab a few spare blankets as we head to the exit.

Outside? It's cold. North Atlantic but only May cold.

"Want to jump first?"

"It's probably freezing - no, no probably. Is that an iceberg?"

There's twenty of us in the raft, everyone huddled together in the cold. Only one man died and a doctor carried him in the raft. I regret not helping out. I mean, isn't there a set of rules on what-to-do-with-corpses?

There's this mother of two bundled together by the spare blankets I grabbed. The kids blow their hands, exaggerated and no doubt learnt in the movies.

I offer the mother my coat.

"No, thank you - you'll freeze to death."

I lift it again, motioning for her to take it from me.

"No, thank you."

"Please."

"No, and if you don't put it back on I'll throw overboard or up your arse."

That wasn't learnt in the movies.

It's been a few hours. Everyone with a digital watch has the face frozen. I hold my old pocket watch to my ear.

"I haven't seen one of those since I got out of the Marines in '79."

I nod.

"I was an Embassy Guard - not in Tehran. Tough times back then: less skirt to chase."

Everyone laughed a little. I'm asking myself if anyone was sane aboard the raft.

"Back then, we could have longer haircuts... man those were the times."

The mother of two looks at me funny then one eye drifts off and down, her arms start twitching as she collapses.

"Mommy's having a seiz-ure."

Morana motions for the little girl.

"Baby, come here. We need you out of the way to save mommy, okay."

The little girl furrows her brow then shrugs it off. She joins Morana. I turn to the older doctor.

"What do we do?"

"Well, we could let it run its course and risk her swallowing her tongue, pin her down head to toe, one person using a stick to press her tongue back."

Morana chimes, "I have a sandfile."

"That'll do."

We gather around the woman, bracing her arms, legs and head. The doctor presses her tongue down. Her movements go for a minute before she passes out, spittle stuck to the corners of her mouth.

"She's going to be alright. Let's keep her warm."

"What's it like?"

"What's what like?"

"A seizure."

"Honestly? I don't remember much except that the more I try to fight, the worse it gets."

By nightfall, everyone slept in a dogpile. The winds blew slow and still, enough to whistle as they passed over every coat and parka.

Morana shifted, unable to sleep.

"Do you think we'll get rescued?"

Mouth pressed to the back of her ear:

"I hope."

She nudges a little closer, pulling my arm around her.

No one tells you how easy it is to fall asleep when you finally get warm. In contrast, everyone acknowledges how difficult it is to get up in the cold.

As a child, my mother loved the outdoors and -when my parents could get away from the restaurant- we'd camp on Mount Diablo. My dad isn't much of a camper.

Mom'd prepare with tents, permits, bug repellent, and a small pickaxe. She wanted us to fit in, in that all-American family way. She wanted that picket fence, single wide in the suburbs. The son playing baseball in high school with a scholarship to a prestigious university.

My father, though distant and stricter, wanted the city. The commotion, the interaction: it interested him. I suppose -despite the overcrowding- the city is more anonymous than the country. You may hide rural but then everyone knows you in town. He wanted the doctor-son who'd take care of his parents in a secluded penthouse, one with his own private practice.

Instead, I'm a short-order cook in the east Atlantic.

An elderly couple sits several feet away. I now realize the wife is crying, not sprayed by the ocean mist.

"Are you alright?"

She looks up, hair held by a crimson beret.

"No, the old bastard's dead."

"What-"

"You're dead. You had to leave me - now! Why?"

She hits him again and again.

"You left me!"

She spits into his face and then hugs him tightly.

"Don't go. Don't go!"

I move over to her.

"Margaret - that's your name right?

"Margaret, he's dead. You have to let go."

She looks up in anger.

"He's gone!"

She gets up slowly, like a child learning how, and walks to edge of the raft. She whispers:

"Horris."

It's then that she jumps as the white caps come crashing.

Morana's head bolts left and she gets up, tossing off the blanket. She just dives into the water after Margaret. Everyone gets up, gathering on the edge of the raft, looking for signs of the old woman. Neither Morana nor she are anywhere to be seen. We wait for a few minutes. No sign.

"Well, it looks like we just lost our third passenger."

I turn around at the doctor and there's something inside of me I haven't felt.

"Don't you say that! Don't you fucking say they're gone!"

I'm worked up. I start tying blankets end to end with square knots. I dive in the water with the blanket tied to my leg.

I don't remember much after this. There was a crimson hat under the water with pale white light and pale white hands. I remember grabbing Morana and then-

I woke up on the raft next to her, stripped of clothes and both us covered like children in swaddling. Margaret is still gone. Morana shivers against me, her wet skin sticking to mine.

"It's all going to be alright," is what I'm meant to say but all that comes out is an exhausted sigh as I rub her shoulders.

The fog set in by early morning. It soaked cloth and ached bones. Waves started picking up, rolling into the raft. We try scooping it out but the water's too cold. It drains slowly through the raft's holes.

All of us are taken back by Margaret's leap. There's a lot you expect in life - this is one of those moments. We tried looking for her but she never surfaced.

I sometimes think she touched the bottom before she passed.

The group argued over what to do with her husband. The children were petrified of his corpse, the unblinking eyes.

"We should put the body overboard," I say, closing the old man's eyelids gently.

"He's not just a body."

"No, but he is dead and the waves are growing. He's extra weight should this raft start sinking."

The mother chimed in, "Don't say that. He's a person."

"If we should sink, are you going to save the weight or the kids?"

She looked off, angry but agreeing. You do what it takes to survive - *what* not being a variable.

The doctor nodded in agreement with me.

With that said, we wrapped his body as best we could. It looked like a cocoon or some misplaced hammock by the time we tied the ends.

"We should say something."

"What do we say?"

Morana gets up and takes my hand:

"Horris - where you go we cannot follow but make your path your own, with Margaret in peace. Amen."

I'm not religious by any stretch but I said amen for the first time in years.

I wish I could say something more eloquent but a boat arrived at half past nine. We almost didn't see it. We heard a horn and thought it an imagination, a figment dangling in our collective head.

When we shook off the shock, we found ourselves smiling but not cheering. We were too tired and cold to jump around on a barely inflated raft. I was surprised only two of had passed through the night but not that they were the oldest.

The children struggled to climb up the mere twenty feet, their shoes slipping but they were braced by the elder passengers. Everyone cold and tired, silently thanking the crew with hugs and smiles.

It was the only warmth summoned in winds five below centigrade.

One by one, we climbed the rickety metal gangplank.

"Do you think it's weird to love someone after twenty-four hours, Chris Tam?"

I look up at Morana. She's facing me at the top of the boat's ladder. Her hair had blown across her face as she pulls it back.

"After the last twenty-four hours, it'd be normal by comparison."

III. History by Numbers: Darren's Story

I stand pointing fingers at the world: blaming the corporations, the government, religion. I have yet to point those finger at myself. The Chai Tea Latte grows cold and less spicy the longer I stand outside in the snows. People dine inside with the earthen accents; the rustic, can-do look that appeals the way an L.L. Bean catalog really shows you know how to "rough it."

Still, I am steeped in what grew more ironic than a latte that is spicier than a straight roast.

I take a drag off the cigarette, flicking it. The embers fly back and hit my trousers smoldering a small hole. *Idiot wind.*

Back in Okinawa, Japan, you could hear my name at every club, in every bar. Go into Kin town -by town, I mean a collection of taverns, all-night restaurants, and tailors for the local military base -you'd probably recognize me. I was the center of the party: cheering in the New Year with my Marines, punching a nasty Army fuck for groping an unwilling female, sloshed against the Shangri-La, lush against Pogue's, spent in Morgan's Irish pub.

Each month I'd gather the younger Marines from work. We'd go to the top of this hill and barbeque until sunset. The beer and champagne would chill on ice while we battered pork rib, steaks, and kielbasa. Lionel showed us how to make a proper shank. I remember writing after one of those drinking nights:

At the Palms,

With drinks patterned,

With their little hats,

People as people and places that rhyme:

34

Sergeants and Corporals
and single malt dry

Staring the sundown
the honchos kill time
-gritting- they sing:

"If only sergeants and corporals
and single malt dry."

I'm a drunk's drunk. There were nine steps before I started drinking. All was well till I got one too many drinks and slept with a local girl. She turned out to belong to a gang and I found myself beaten the next day, missing formation and marching the Battalion color guard. I had beaten two of them but no charges were filed. They busted me down but did not bust me out.

That's the version that's flattering to me.

They say the President hears when a Marine breaks the law in Japan. Leave it to me to break five but get away scot flying free. All of this took place after I left a mental hospital, after Iraq, after a failed marriage, after the point of it all.

I'm pushing carts in a grocer's parking lot, relishing the forty-degree rains that bolster Seattle's suicide rate.

It's been several months since I left the Marine Corps. My hair barely rests on my shoulders now and my goatee is scruffier than one of Kurt Cobain's flannel sweaters.

So, I'm pushing these carts and counting the yellow ribbons emblazoned with "Support Our Troops". There's nothing like putting a 99 cent decal on your fat fucking SUV to show patriotism.

Well-intentioned fuckers.

There's talk of us protecting freedom: of dying for it.

But freedom to do what?

We live in a nation where Paris Hilton and Anna Nicole Smith were national icons, eating up the evening news.

We live in nation primping in front of a mirror: tweezing eyebrows to succinct little lines, applying cover-up, and praying to God that no one finds out you have hair on your body. Heaven forbid you look like a normal person. Heaven forbid you have pubic hair.

And I'm condemning the world: having just finished my Mocha Frappucino and Wendy's fries but it doesn't excuse our national obsession with finding the g-spot when we can't even find Iraq on a map.

Adjusting to life outside of the military wasn't that hard. I'd been to college before I joined. The only difficulty was rebuilding that circle of friends you lose once you leave. Everyone comes in from all walks of life and Marines all leave the same: back to disparate directions and routes unknown from when they started.

Sarah was the first person I met when I took the job at Glouster's two years ago. I found her writing "fuck the system - happy b-day" on Gretchen's windshield with L'Oreal's Cherry Freeze lipstick.

That was the introduction.

"What are you doing?"

She turned her head toward me, still crouched on the vehicle's hood.

"That's a pretty lame question unless you can't read."

"What?"

"The name's Sarah, yours?"

"Sergeant Kitlor."

"Sergeant?"

Realizing I'd just introduced myself like I was back in the Marines, I corrected:

"Darren, the name's Darren."

"What branch of service were you in?"

"Marine Corps."

"My father was in the Army - twenty-five years. Don't worry about it - he did the same thing when he got out."

- - -

I return to my flat.

I keep things tidy. I can't focus in a messy room. There's a nagging feeling that I'm wasting time on the computer, typing a blog or playing a game.

Instead, my messes reside in a secretary, a closeted desk. Notebooks line the shelves around my computer. Old stuff I wrote in college, in the Corps, and… that's where it ends.

I haven't written something worthwhile in years.

I drop a book bag on the wood floor, kicking a trash can full of homeless ideas aside.

"Daren, Darren, Darren."

That's what comes out my mouth as I slap my forehead.

Write, write. My fingers just dance a hair's breadth above the keyboard, the way Marie Antoinette might have watched the Russian Opera. For all its grace, it lacks any substance. Nothing is coming from these fingers, except the middle one I point at the ceiling.

"Hello world. I hate you, just like the previous sentence and its mind-numbing mediocrity to the average programmer.

There's a confession I have to make.

All is not well in the land of photogenic shopping isles and pristine white floors. The perfect stacks of cans with their concentric circles, the precise waves of the buffed floor: all of this an illusion for you. The upbeat, quick music is designed to make you impulsive and cheerful, optimistic that the fifty dollar prosciutto is better than the bargain brand at others stores.

There's a croissant for you, a horn. There's a chance you're being cheated.

My girlfriend says I must be cheating. We started dating months ago, exclusively online. She started a fight, last night.

Her reason: I am cold and distant after having sex.

Well, no shit, we're dating on-line."

- - -

I finished a cart pull and went inside. Our grocery store uses this giant fan entrance instead of a door. It has this tendency to suck the dress slacks into the grill. I still get caught when I wear my loose pair of slacks.

Tom, a regular customer, and Sarah are in the middle of discussion.

"What's so funny?"

"Oh, Tom here was telling me about this guy at his work. He asked if he knew President Obama."

"Aren't you from Chicago?"

"Well, deal is - he didn't know that, he thought I was raised here."

"Ri-ight. I guess he thought all black people know each other - like they all came from his granddaddy's plantation."

"I know - right," Tom laughs.

I turn to Sarah.

"Hey, I have an extra ticket to the Nine Inch Nails concert Friday. Yes, no?"

"So long as it's not a date, dear sir."

"Deal."

- - -

Sarah wound up enjoying the concert. We stayed in the pit for the first half of the show, before the hooligans re-energized and could crush her against the barricade. We stayed by the backstage exit afterwards, long enough to see Trent Reznor come out. Sarah asked him to sign her t-shirt.

The drive back from Seattle took less time than we imagined, so we stopped off at Denny's. Denny's at one in the morning is the best. Its science: we took a poll and it came back yes.

We wound up getting drunk and ordering breakfast platters. The conversation consisted of strung-together epithets, strung-out discussions on each of our favorite interests, and strung-on non-sequiturs leading us to taking shots of Tabasco till the bill arrived.

Sarah and I wound up crashing in my car: I got front, she got backseat.

- - -

Sarah yawns, stretching her arms as her shirt rides up her midriff. She bends her head over lackadaisically. That is, until she looks at her watch. Each of us have shift in two hours. It's an hour drive to get home and we both smell like burnt pubic hair, old sweat, and taquitos.

"Don't worry, we didn't do anything," she says, rolling over. Her eyes are bloodshot and her eyeliner a bit runny. I reach over to rub the smudge off her cheeks.

"That's a shame. I would've *so* let you take me."

She rolls her eyes at the comment and points to the highway.

"Drive."

- - -

"Hurry up, Sarah. We're going to be late. Don't be using my razor either, that thing's strictly for my face."

"Yeah, yeah, yeah," she laughs from my flat's tiny 0.5 bathroom. Wish we could be like the English and call it a water closet - which is closer to the truth given my square footage.

Sarah comes out already wearing her cardigan but missing one vital element: pants.

I cover my eyes in fake protest.

"They're on the door knob. You didn't hear?"

"No. Next time you'd better be louder or you're never getting a peep show again."

"Well, I'll be certain to yell."

She raises her middle finger at me and sticks out her tongue.

- - -

The second time we went out to Iraq, our Intel guys said not to travel east toward Karbala from Al Anbar. Our Platoon commander gave the order, with the prospect of seeing an old friend from The Basic School. Sure enough, 3rd Intel Battalion gave good information when we radioed. The bombs went off near a horse carcass on the side of the road. The first struck the MRC-142, our radio vehicle. Ramirez, if he felt anything at all, drove that one. They'd discover it a full mortar round stuffed into the thing. 2nd Lieutenant Kurich was blown to safety in the sand mounds to the right. Not a limb left his body.

This wasn't his first time either. He'd led us the wrong direction on patrol once as well; three died. Three men died so his college educated ass could earn a Bronze Star without a "V" for valor. You see, he got so lost he saw none of the shooting. He wasn't there when Lance Corporal Petrus fell, nor when Tony -a Private for life and friendly loquacious guitarist- took a RPG tearing his legs clean off.

No, the Lieutenant didn't see that. We found him hunched over in a house later, claiming to have been getting a vantage point to fight. None of us approached him then.

When we got back to 29 Palms, I started drinking harder - showing up to work with cheeks rosy but my work ethic harder than ever. They say there's a thing as a functional drunk - it's true but only one with a chip on his shoulder. There's this concept of a line of departure: the moment where there's no turning back and you're in it thick.

Our Lieutenant was to be presented that day with that medal.

I had stood watch the day prior and had the day off. Nothing to do but sit and drink on the second story, over-watching the formation where some heroes, some sinners. None of us were saints but only one of us cost the lives of ten men: young men with futures. Ramirez had planned on starting an auto repair shop when he got out in three years. They held a closed casket service for him. Promoted 1st Lieutenant Kuric spoke to his parent's after the funeral: he said how greatly he respected and admired Ramirez. His family cried and hugged him. Kurich had gotten to the unit the before we started training for our second Iraq outing. He barely knew Ramirez, a quiet, former stoner with a deep love for his wife.

So, when they called the names, I walked down to watch from the sidelines. He stands there all beaming like a child on parade. I smash my bottle of Guinness and walk into the formation. No one does anything, the whole battalion at attention with full military discipline. The commander and sergeant major don't even see me go at Lieutenant. I went up him, shank in hand wanting to desperately point it at his neck.

I spent a night in the brig before getting sent to Bethesda, Maryland.

I spent three weeks in a psychiatric ward after that. It's a exercise in futility to explain how normal it is to feel bad when you've lost a third of your platoon to enemy IEDs planted along the roadside in Al-Anbar province.

I say badly when I should say something like morose or depressed.

In our patient groups, we pass around this little sheet with cartoon characters making faces with associated emotions. There's one for happy, one for meditative, one for discombobulated. There's not one for patronized or talked down to.

We pass it around and state our name, why we're here, our goal for treatment that day, and how we feel.

Good morning, my name is Darren Kitlor, Marine Corps. I'm here for post-traumatic stress disorder and depression. My goal is to get out of here. I am numb.

Of course, I don't say "get out of here". That's a vague goal, you have to have something quantifiable like draw two pictures or call family.

In the ward, I met a young Vietnamese soldier. She attempted suicide after taking an entire bottle of Tylenol followed by her Lunesta. She had long black hair when she let it down. She'd just made it to her job school. Her family had immigrated when she was a baby. Her mother was a hairdresser, owning a salon out in East Los Angeles. This bright, beautiful girl couldn't find a reason worth living.

I taught her a song on the piano, an arrangement of "A Warm Place" with work for both hands. She picked it up quickly, learning each hand before combining the two. It probably made it easier as I learnt the whole thing at once, struggling through it at college and sneaking into the piano conservatory on campus. She could play it quite well by the time she was discharged.

We didn't speak much, just listening to each other in the other room during group therapy sessions, tracking the others' progress.

"Why did you attempt suicide, Darren?" she asked, tinkering with the keys. All I could do was stare out the window onto Rockville Pike. I didn't say much, so inured by my own experiences and still uncomfortable with the prospect of my own mortality.

"I did it because I felt like a failure."

"A failure? You're a corporal though."

"I know but the novelty wears off once you get past training."

"What did you fail at?"

"Well..."

- - -

It's my second deployment to Iraq. The sand comes up during a storm, winds licking at the loose fabric of our uniforms. The glare off the sun visors distracts me.

I'm counting the number of steps I take today. It's a game. We've played it before: days so bored you count the holes in the saltine crackers in the Meal Ready-to-Eat; the days you mix the entire contents of tobacco and grape jelly to eat with that jalapeno cheese spread.

We get bored and tired on countless patrols, kicking in door after door. There is no reprieve during a foot patrol. In the open, a foot patrol would be welcome: you could see the enemy. In the city, it's a nightmare.

We're not in vehicles. Humvees are more vulnerable than our own skins. A roadside bomb went off this morning, sometime after Lance Corporal Ramirez went out. Huge explosion. I heard he was there.

He's from an L.A. suburb, his wife having given birth this past month. He managed a satellite call two months before the delivery. He's yet to see the child. He drinks too much but he works hard. He'll follow an order.

So, when the bomb went off, I thought of the box he left at the foot of his rack. The box with that letter he wrote home to his wife. There are many letters but this one is shortest of all. It does not ask how the Navy-Marine Corps Relief Society is bailing their month's rent. It does not discuss his in-laws who are still leery of Hispanic blood in the family.

It is a letter without a planned date to mail. It is the letter not submitted during mail call.

It is not a suicide letter. It reads the same but it is not. I did not read it but I've imagined what we all write. I wish I could be a better husband, father, brother, son, lover. It's obscenely personal, piously pornographic, and deeply familial. You don't read these letters: there's a thing as too much intimacy.

There are days where we unload vehicles and load them again, just for practice, just to pass time. We bitch. We're experts at bitching and pretend to understand why we clean our weapons for hours and clean the sand from open-air tents. We "understand" why we paint a freshly painted vehicle again.

It's boredom and anonymity that costs us lives, not hajjis in checkered head wraps. It's bombs without clear makers, stupid accidents that we vow never to make: it is faceless and -for all the shouting and flag burning- does not care.

Gunfire ricochets in the distance. It isn't sustained. It could be Iraqi kids, holding a weapon high in the air. You see them running up in tattered Teenage Mutant Ninja Turtle t-shirts. Clothes from your youth that made their way over here, sometime before the sanctions. Dirty little faces with polka dotted teeth and good spirits. They'll wave and run alongside the vehicle.

The sound could be burning ammunition. A mortar strike hit here just hours before we dismounted the vehicles. You can see the smoke, burning black oil off a car.

I raise my rifle and crouch.

You can hear another IED go off in the distance and I stand reminded.

When we return from patrol, I will mail Ramirez's letter.

- - -

I was surprised by how attached I grew to Private Phoung. Call it a co-dependent nightingale effect. Call it Stockholm syndrome in a place where they confiscate the slightest piece of metal on your person.

When she left, I gave her a big hug and said I wanted to hear her playing that song in twenty years. She smiled and left, not turning back on such a sad place. We didn't exchange email addresses; we never spoke.

When it came time for art therapy, I drew a picture of Ramirez, Phoung, and others. We were all children dressed in pajamas on a playground, tussling in a pig pile. Everyone smiling and struggling; yanking and pulling. Everyone felt like strands in a larger rope, woven together like the pig pile. For all our differences, all our autonomy, we still relied on each other for strength-

-and I failed Ramirez. I failed him when I didn't speak up during the convoy brief, I failed when I didn't finish the job on that two-bit Lieutenant, I failed when I lost my luggage on return to the States – never able to deliver his final letter to his wife.

I vowed to tell her when I got out, vowed to tell his wife how much he cared for her, how he spoke in high regard of her father -despite his racism-.

You see, you're a member of a larger family in the military. You take care of the man or woman next to you. It's simple: Us v. Them.

Still, I failed Ramirez, having lost that letter. The closest thing to family since my mother past to leukemia when I entered my senior year of high school, before I hit the streets and had to strike out my own place for college.

I failed Ramirez.

I don't have family outside my Marines, my wife not counting. She left with a fellow Marine stationed back in 29 Palms, California, months before we returned.

They met at the Marine Corps Exchange - the shopping centers that remind our troops of small town strip malls all across the world. That transplanted bit of the American dream.

She met him there of all places. They saw each other for five of the seven months I was over there, long enough to send divorce paperwork out to me. Long enough for me to be med-evacuated through Landstuhl, Germany.

We married right after I got out of boot camp. I was young; she was younger and available. She came from a Deming, a logging town up highway 9, north of Sedro-Woolley, another logg- I'll stop when you can detect a theme. She'd had a kid from high school when we met. It didn't matter. The kid was cute and meant a lot to me. Jimmy, with his one good leg, his mother being a drinker during and after the pregnancy.

As for infidelity, I couldn't judge her. I'd fooled around myself and perhaps she knew. It didn't matter. I knew it was happening. It's not one of those things where you feel better for saying you did it first.

She didn't tell me and I never returned to 29 Palms again. She just stopped returning my calls three months in. Not a peep from the scuffed AT&T phone card at the air station in Iraq, not a word when we returned. She just vanished up into thin air. I suppose the desert swallowed her like it did everyone else I knew.

So, when the doctors ask if that made me feel angry or sad, I want to reach across the table. *Of course it does. Wouldn't you feel it? What type of question is that to ask?*

- - -

I'm in a dream.

The dawn paints the whiteboard in colors you could imagine drinking, making my handwriting stand-out. The marker rests in my hand. Black splotches climb up the side of my hands, freckles from exposure to too many words.

I'm teaching French at some university. That's the thing about dreams, the way that things intuitively come to you. There's no logic or explanation. In a dream, you speak Parisian French fluently.

The ink melts with the sunrise. Ink bleeds down the sterile surface, clouding the yellows, oranges, and reds.

Where it once read a passage from Camus it now reads, "La meilleure chose au sujet de la vie est de savoir comment vous avez mis ensemble."

My arms flail up and down, my head shaking. I try to stop. I try to flex but the muscles are already tense. It's an epileptic fit, the hands jump and prance across the board, erasing the letters and writing ones in their place.

My face hits the board and I cough up ink. It's running down my lips. The last thing I see is my body staring into the board. There are no words left, just dress shoe black caked across.

And the classroom seats are vacant, the world outside covered in sixteen feet of pure, white snow.

- - -

It's killing me.

Sarah's eating a cup of noodles, wicking the yellow broth off the corners of her mouth with the tip of her pinky finger. Her hair is pulled back and there's this intense look in her eye.

She's like that reading the paper.

Our uniforms are that only in spirit: her pink neck scarf serves counterpoise to a mandatory black cardigan. She stopped wearing make-up months ago-

-and now she's staring off into space.

I search her eyes, watching the pupils sitting motionless in a deep blue sea, tethered by some unknown force.

"Are you alright?"

She takes a second to shake the distant look.

"Yeah - I'm fine."

She smiles wide but crooked.

- - -

I convinced myself that Triple Distilled Vodka, Bailey's, and Kalahua were my muse when I got back from Iraq.

I tried so very carefully to not appear drunk but my head spun with lights flashing. Life looks over-exposed, the lens open too long. Everything is stop-motion photography and my head races around its track.

I fumble with the lock, like a lover's first time figuring out the fish-hook of a girl's brassiere. All pinky fingers and dangling keys.

I'm not sure how much longer I can keep this up. I don't know. It feels weird saying I'm past my prime as I near my 26th birthday but I'm feeling it - feeling it fierce.

Life's a pyramid on end: your options and the world wide open at the start and gradually narrowing till you are what you are. I grew up thinking I could be a paleontologist, a doctor, a FBI agent, etc. All people do.

My 27th birthday is the 21st of next month and I realize how concretely I don't have those options anymore. I'm barely going to finish college at this rate. *Where to from there?* I'm used up, spent. I've heard a lot of "well, that's life" from myself and others, settling down to its inevitabilities. Do we choose or merely wind up in our niche? Are we creators or created by our circumstance? Whatever it is, I don't have a clue anymore and I'm getting tired of thinking about it.

I see what they mean when they say the sun is a star in someone else's sky.

I need to get clean, to clean myself and clean my closet. All the whoring in Europe, the drinking till blackout in Okinawa, the coin slots of the Palms: all of them felt load-some, like a rucksack after a ten mile hump.

- - -

Once, in the weeks leading up to Christmas, I pranked Sarah and -in turn- pranked the local mall. We were walking by the food court, the same ones that exist in every mall with the Orange Julius, the McDonald's, and that same short-order Asian express: all reminders of how cheap and available food is available here in America. Anything beat the years of ready to eat meals in the chilling cold of north Iraq.

We got to the open space and I stopped, getting down on one knee.

"What the fuck are you doing?"

"Just go with it," I whispered.

I turned my head and loudly announce my intentions,

"Ladies and gentlemen."

People stop and take notice.

I grab her hands and pull a small velvet box from my pocket.

Everyone is staring now. Who proposes in a food court? Who are these people?

I lean in close to Sarah and whisper:

"Will you take the ring to Mordor with me?"

She turns her head away, trying to keep from laughing.

"Yes!" she says, adding a barely audible, "You fucker."

I jump up to my feet and people are clapping. A middle-aged man cheers.

I kiss her quickly, consummating the prank.

- - -

The psychiatrist in Bethesda tells me I have a Major Depressive Disorder.

The worst part about depression is not the self-loathing but the associated insomnia. People say it must be great to not need to get some sleep. That's disingenuous. Your body needs sleep, whether you get it or not.

Take your average day for example. Take the number of times you're bored: whether you get drowsy or yawn or feel restless. Now add eight hours to your day. It's not like you can do anything more productive. Sure, you could write or get another job but you'd just be extending those hours of boredom. You cannot be entertained in a regular day, let alone 24/7.

The doctor also says I have PTSD.

That's his way of saying I'm unfit for continued military service. It's saying, "hey, the shit you saw was bad and you can't deal with." I mean, how do you deal with it? Is there a guidebook somewhere that says this is what you should feel when your friends die, your wife cheats, and you get hit by improvised explosive device. There isn't one. I trust psychiatrists with my life but sometimes it must be frustrating, even for them, to acknowledge that there isn't a set routine for all of life's behaviors. If you could boil life down, it'd be chaos. It'd be stuff x, y, and z led to b. There's no one cause but infinite causes to what happens in life and for such, you can only choose actions, not the consequences that follow.

He says I should have full VA benefits upon leaving: the Montgomery GI Bill, disability pay, even health care when I leave.

My first thought was that I didn't deserve those things.

My second: what am I supposed to do on the outside? I'm trained to fight, born to kill, ready to die, now knowing I will.

- - -

My problems were small in comparison to some. All I had was a bottle, some anger, and a dose of self-loathing.

It was a rainy day in autumn that Sarah confessed to me. She'd been clean for a month she said. She lifted the sleeves of her cardigan slowly, showing me her arms and you could make out the faint white scars from past needle tracks.

"Jesus, Sarah."

Her eyes shot away at the comment and I realized that being stunned only drove things deeper.

"I never stopped to ask why you always wore sweaters."

Her lip was quivering but tears weren't coming out.

"Now you know."

Some feet were making their way upstairs and Sarah tossed her arm underneath mine, interlocking our fingers. For all the scars she now hid under my arm, she felt like cotton quilts, ones embroidered with little reminders up and down the seams. We looked into each others' eyes for a good long while.

"What do you think of me?"

"I -"

I just put my arm around her and held her tight.

"I've got to go."

- - -

"You thought about the consequences of dating your best friend?"

"Yes, I'm not retarded."

Michael looks up, creasing his eyebrows.

"Okay - maybe a little retarded."

"That's better."

"So, what do I do?"

"Listen - I can't tell you what to do. If I were you, I'd probably risk it but just know the risks involved."

"It's not like people stop being friends when one tells the other the other they love them."

"Not immediately, no."

"Next chance, I'm telling her."

- - -

There's a steady drum from the bass inside. Sarah sits beneath the loading bay flood lights, on the ledge, her feet rocking a shopping cart through the slush.

In Seattle, it doesn't rain so much as it melts. Hell doesn't freeze over so much as sublime.

It's not so bad though: I only wear a thin jacket.

Sarah smokes a cigarette, rolling her sleeves down her fingers till the thumb disappears in the black cardigan.

It's New Year's Eve and London's calling the rest of the night crew back into the bay. This is the one night a year we refuse shipments. It's as easy as skating. The center store manager sits in the back of the room, cutting the Christmas roses. He's been trying to avoid looking at Sarah.

It's hard really. As much as she resents it, she is attractive. That's where I stop. I never mentioned it to her after she brushed me off and punch my shoulder. I think she didn't expect those words from me.

I'm outside though, talking to Sarah as she sits on the ledge between the two dozen employees sharing spiced rum punch and little nut-covered cheese balls and the empty back lot. Sarah and I don't feel like dancing to Top 40 hits. Neither of us particularly wants a "sexy back" right now. She rests her chin on her palm. Her cigarette rests next to her cheek as she hunches over. She breaks another daze before smiling at me. The eyes just shift out of focus, toward the tree-line and free-way beyond.

I roll a few mounds of snow, forming a ball.

"Don't you dare, sir."

I look up, my breath obscuring her cigarette smoke.

"Or what?"

She sticks her tongue out and it's just then that I toss it. The impact is soft but turns her cheeks that newborn pink. Her shining mouth is open, half-smiling and half grimaced, arms out like a crucifix.

"Fucker."

That's the term of endearment she grants Darren. Not punk or idiot: not terms she uses when genuinely mad. Fucker:

one who fucks. See also Fuck. Etymological origins unknown. See also sexual intercourse.

That's what a college education gets you when you drop out, useless facts mixing over tongue. I try hard not to talk about the origins of the word, not now, not when I actually want to talk.

"Sarah."

She looks up cigarette still grasped between knuckles.

"Yes?" Her tone rings playful.

Here's that moment I've dreamt of: saying "I love you." We've said it platonically long enough. I love her the way adults do. I'm afraid I'll come off more like van Gough than don Juan: another friendship ruined by definitions and expectations of what two people should do about those pesky XX/XY chromosomes. That biological urge that sustained millennia of hunter gatherers on the plains of Africa. Yes, those urges but something deeper, something purer than instinct itself. I cared her, really cared for her. I couldn't imagine a world without her. The way she gathered her hair or tagged cars with lipstick when they took her spot. I loved her ability to break down my garrulous diction and find out what troubles me when I go off on a tirade on universal health care and corporate involvement.

"I love you."

She smiles and chokes a little on her smoke.

"I do too. You're a good friend."

Good friend. I'm relegated to that level. The nice guy, suffocating in his own sweater. For once, I wish I were more than just that. As shallow and trite and pretentious as it is, I wish I were more: more than the sex appeal of Mister Rogers, more than love's labor's kindly dismissed with four words.

"Not just a friend."

She takes a last puff of the cigarette before flicking it aside. On her feet, Sarah's fast - a sprinter in High School. She punches me in the arm.

"Quite teasing, fucker," she laughs.

"Really - is that it," I say, we're inching closer.

"Yeah, that's it."

My palms are sweating and it's 21 degrees outside. It's now or never. I lean into kiss her and our lips brush. There's the start of her lips pressing back and then a hand pushes on my chest. She turns away.

"I can't."

Her eyes are downturned and she pulls back her hair.

"How do you feel?"

"How am I supposed to feel? Jesus, Darren. What am I supposed to say to that? Did you think you'd just disembowel yourself?"

IV.   History By Numbers: Sarah's Story

Sarah realized how much that hurt. She didn't hate him. This cruelty was new and unexpected to her relationship with him.

"You're drunk. Just go home, forget about it."

She doubted the first part herself - he'd claimed to have given up drinking after admitting to his problem. She'd fought tooth and nail to get him to share a glass of Vodka and Bailey's at the diner after the concert. She couldn't expect him to do the second part either, not when she wouldn't be forgetting about it herself.

"Why - why, Sarah?"

She pauses, breath dissipating into the Christmas lights from the farms across the road. I'm just stunned and it cuts - like warm knife and butter.

"Why?!?!"

She threw her cigarette into a puddle of half-dissolved seafood ice.

She couldn't. *Where do you start? How could he know what it's like to be strung out during her own mother's funeral, too blazed to even answer the phone? Would he sympathize when she fell into the memory of a bad trip? How do you convey the feelings, unfolding into each other: the disgust, desperation, and remorse when -naked- she rolled over, after fucking a now sleeping dealer for an ounce? You couldn't.*

I'm fat. Maybe I should call him. He's willing to settle with a fat "chick". No, I'm not fat. I just have a drug problem. Great - you have a guy with a junkie fetish admitting his love to you. Does he know? No, he couldn't. There's no possible way. Why do people use chick anyways? Are young women some sort of defenseless yellow bird? No, I didn't think so. What does that make men? Cocks? Chick-lets? Maybe I'm not fat but I do have a drug problem. I should eat. Admitting love? Is this a courthouse? Where is the judge, the jury? I don't have many friends.

I'd have more if I wasn't blowing my money on porcelain. Maybe I should eat some oatmeal. That's good. How am I going to make this month's rent? Oatmeal has less fat, it promotes a healthy heart. Great, now I'm stealing sayings off the side of food packaging. Why does he love me?

For all his worldly travels, Darren is the least worldly man she knew. He didn't curse out-loud, didn't smoke. So, he might be an alcoholic - she agreed not to judge his situation. It wasn't smack. No, if Darren were a sinner, he'd be St. Peter.

She admired the way he treated women. Once -during a smoke break- he brought in carts from the side lot. A young man and his girlfriend were walking by. The girl held her engorged stomach with one arm, the other gripped above the wrist by her boyfriend.

"Tony. Slow down, the baby's kicking."

He ignored her, clearly furious with that wild look in his eye.

"Tony..." Her voice trailed off taking a high-pitched, nasal quality, one of resignation.

He turned to her and raised a hand.

"Listen, bitch -"

As his hand raised to slap her, Darren jumped over the hedges.

"Excuse me, sir? Is this your child?"

Darren pointed to the girl's stomach. The boyfriend didn't know what to make of such a question.

"Yes?!"

Darren punched him - with his rear hand.

The boyfriend staggered back a bit, shook and blinked into the lights.

"Don't talk to the mother of your child that way. Just do your business and leave."

Darren walked out, nonchalant, to return the shopping cart tether to the parcel storage room. He tored off his hat, frustrated with the boyfriend.

Before he could enter the swinging door, Sarah grabbed him by the parka.

"Darren -"

She looked at him and he looked back, eyes now calm and soft again. There was this pause and he put his hand to her cheek.

She couldn't tell him then either.

This dichotomy between him and her: the tug of war between the wants of the heart and the desire to give the other a better life. This struggle is why Sarah needed to say it:

"Darren, I don't love you."

She'd told the only man she loved to shove off. Things loomed disproportionately as she entered her house. How could she have a normal life? Instead of being a burden to a lover, wasn't a partner the thing she needed?

There were days that she wondered what his mouth tasted like. The night he punched the boyfriend it smelled of strawberries and ginger, from a cereal he'd eaten on break. He leant over one night on the couch and his breath smelled of mango and fresh popcorn. She would wonder what he looked like without his shirt, aside from glances she snuck when he painted the exceptionally tall corners of the drywall in her house. His lanky body was fine and sinewy, defined and soft around the edges. He had a nice stomach, even if she preferred bulkier men

-but he wasn't hers and could never be.

Her mind like a ferry's props churned under the waves of reasoning that she spat out in the wake. Darren deserved a woman his equal, she mused. A woman smart and refined. For all his talk of empowering women and hating smart women who retired to marriage, he did deserve someone who'd sacrifice herself like.

But why? What did he see in her? Her thin, china skin: opaque and bluish, Her ratty black hair, split and fried. A venomous tongue that put his Marine associates to shame. A disgust with sex -with decent men- after years of acquiring her vice.

Everything in its right place: he in his, she in hers.

Her tears didn't grow as she rationalized. They just dried under the weight of common sense. Of self-doubt in half-truths. She felt as if her body were on autopilot. Every limb moved on its own accord, like legs after running on a treadmill. She was watching herself in third person.

Soon, she'd get some burritos from Taco Bell and -

Soon, she'd call Marc and -

Soon, they'd discuss the cost of six ounces of Judas and -

Soon, he would drive over and remove her bra and she'd wouldn't have to feel -

Soon.

Marc came quickly, pulling up in his German import. He could afford to. His carefully tweezed eyebrows and spiced cologne gave every impression but that of a small time dealer. His clothes were always in style, the woven shirts and slacks from places like Ibiza and Milan. The man never wore jeans.

His hair had the habit of always being "just" so, that tedious look of trying not to be styled. His features were sharp but not caricatures: strong and memorable and masculinely defined.

But above all this, he knew he looked good - and used it well.

Sarah let him in. He wrapped an arm around the front of her waist and she now felt ill at the prospect of sleeping with him. The prices he gave her were not reasonable otherwise. She shuddered, from the small of her back to the base of her head. She couldn't sleep with him. It would only exacerbate the pangs she felt.

Marc set his automatic Zippo on the table: followed by a finely polished spoon and sterile wrapped needles. He did out-calls for his clientele. It lowered the risk they'd be strung out in public, allowed him to charge more, and -he felt pleased with himself- what cop expects the dealer to make house calls with an ounce - a misdemeanor?

It benefited and protected him, a rarity in his field.

"Remove your cardigan, lift your blouse."

Sarah did so hesitantly, she wanted to talk him out and find another form of payment.

"Don't worry. It's the needle that bites, not me."

Marc ignited the Zippo, dissolving the heroin obviously cut with a little lactic powder. He unpackaged a syringe, drained a healthy dose and flicked the air bubbles to one end of the syringe, then squeezed it out. He leant over and kissed her inner elbow.

She drew a sharp breath as it went and rolled her head over to face the Christmas lights still up next door.

"Happy New Year."

Using heroin is like being wrapped in swaddling cloth for the first time. You may go kicking and screaming through the world: cold, alone, and in pain. Heroin is like wrapping that first blanket -that warm cotton- all around then getting nestled against your mother's breasts, nudging your head to make room and falling asleep.

It is at the same time better than any orgasm you've ever experienced minus the muscle tension, sweaty hands, and having to worry about what to talk about afterwards.

Sarah could've blamed an abusive father who had molested her as a child. She could. No one would blame her. She couldn't speak to him at all. Every time she saw him as a kid she'd tense up and freeze: a deer in that unblinking gaze of his.

She could blame that. The court doctors determined there "wasn't a significant level of damage to her labial tissue beyond what aggressive sports might cause to a seven year old."

She could blame her mother, a lush -if not total alcoholic-. Her mother would sit and watch soap operas all day. In various states of consciousness she curse her daughter and then turn the volume higher. Her mother was thirty-eight. Again, she could place it on that.

In the end, Sarah didn't put the blame on anyone but herself. She liked how it felt, like the way the blood would back a little into the syringe then expel through the dropper's neck. She liked the way the blood flowed, how it took less than a second for it to hit and then-

-she'd feel good. This is why she did it. Everyone wants to feel better about themselves, fell more confident, more comfortable. You felt successful while on it. It was the American dream in an ounce.

The grounds outside are covered in snow: all delicate and powdered.

Yet it feels like déjà vu of last year, the year before, and the year the birthed that one too.

She grabbed her purse, trying to apply make-up in the car's side mirrors. Sarah smashed the rearview a few months back and had to throw away the make-up case's mirror. She had to. Mirrors with their insinuating glances: the way those jealous eyes of mine stare. The reminders of what she used them for: not to look at herself but to look away, to get away from the world. Three snow drifts at a time.

I give up. It's a routine I've tried for months.

The snow stuck then disappeared against her black sweater. The way wool clung when wet, that bristly cold. It left puddles across the surface of the skin. Like pin-pricks.

I don't need anyone to tell me I'm not a cat. A moan escaped her lips as a man offered Sarah a cart. He winked.

She accepted it and wait till he's gone to put it back in the lot. I don't need it. I work here. For all the déjà vu, it's as if no one noticed.

"Cunt waffle."

This woman goes through Sarah's lane, angry at her slow hands and cursing that all her courtesy was in vain.

"I'm late thanks to you. Maybe when you get a real job, you'll understand."

She looks at my ring finger.

"Some of us don't have as many people counting on them."

She grabs her things forcefully. You can tell the difference after a while: good people never toss their eggs.

As soon as she left, Sarah closed her eyes.

"Fuck."

"You alright, Sarah?"

"Yeah."

There's a lull in the queue.

"Darren!" Sarah calls out.

"What do you want?"

"Don't take that tone - check your bike."

Darren went outside to collect the carts again and looked at his old Schwinn. The snows were getting pretty deep and they'd probably close the store tomorrow - something not seen save for the day after Christmas for the annual inventory.

Three snowmen stood around his bicycle: one wore a blue scarf with the produce section's baby carrots for a nose, another wore a hunting cap -all mangled and molted-, while the last-

-the last snowman was decapitated by the bicycle, its head and body on either side.

Darren smiled and drew his hood around his face.

How am I going to make this month's rent? As it is, I'm already down to a subsistence of chicken thighs and rice. You can feed yourself for twenty dollars a week on a bag of rice: twenty dollars will buy butter, milk, chicken. It's all you really need.

She'd been on such a diet for so long that she couldn't tell if she were gaining weight or just more undernourished. Her cabinets were bare, all dried and cleaned out.

This problem isn't going away.

Her account was over-drafted again meaning she'd have to go hungry a week, scraping the cupboards bare, before her new card arrived. Another week and no change. Broke and without love. It marked another year since she sought emancipation from her parents. Another year of shooting up and selling herself to her dealer. I will never be free if I keep this up.

She started to cry. As child, she'd bullied the other kids on the playground. She once made a boy eat dirt for calling her a dog. She spent the next week in detention, defiant and knowing that they couldn't keep her there forever. She was right - or as right as a third grader can be.

All in all, she was not a crier. She stormed into the bathroom. Alone, she took out a small pouch from the inner pocket of her cardigan. Inside was the upper half of a silver spoon, a fresh 22s gauge needle, and a little teabag glued up.

She took the spoon out and opened the teabag, cutting her finger on the corner. Taking out a lighter, she flicked it on and held the spoon over top, cleaning it out by fire. Pouring a little of the chalky powder in, she began cooking it. It bubbled and chortled as it formed a brown viscous fluid. The needle went it once the granules dissipated. Sucking it up, she tapped it and got the air bubbles toward the needle's head, squirting it out.

She tied her cardigan around her arm as tight as she could, clenching her fist to make the veins bulge. It wasn't hard for her. Her pale, cream-colored skin made the bluesy lines look like highways on some distant map. The drug was her cure, the ability to stoic-up whenever she wanted. You don't have to worry about pain or joy, loneliness or love: just the needle and its neck.

She then withdrew a small portion of blood from the site before injecting, sealing the deal and-

-                            .

Sarah woke to cold vomit on her bathroom floor. The sink ran and overflowed. Lukewarm water reached her bottom lip, chunks of partially digested food floating in it. *Am I awake? Am I alive?* She tried moving her arm but it felt removed, as if a million miles away. Reaching a numb hand into her pocket, she takes out her cell phone. Blue fingertips hit the number:

- . . . please.

65

Darren sat at home when his cell phone rang. It was Sarah. *I don't want to speak to you. Just leave me alone.* The phone rang and rang until it finally went silent. *What if she wants to talk? Of course, she wants to talk. What if it's work? What if it's her parents? What if...*

He sat for another five minutes before the what-ifs grew too much to bear and he went outside to ride his bike.

When he arrived, he saw the lights on but no one home. He peered through the window and something on the floor. It was Sarah, covered in white frothy vomit, blood leaking from a cut on her forehead.

Darren broke in through the front door. It reminded him of the first time he went on patrol. Fallujah stomping in the sandbox.

Sarah lay there motionless on the floor. Darren rolled her onto her side, letting the vomit drain from her mouth, leg bent forward to hold her in place.

He checked her neck for a pulse. Nothing but the feel of her skin. Darren jumped on top, straddling her and started chest compressions.

"One - one hundred, two - one hundred..."

The ambulance came quickly. Darren had revived her but only to semi-consciousness. She mumbled incoherently as they lifted her frail body onto the stretcher. He rode with them to the hospital, able to decipher her mumbling better than the medical jargon thrown back and force. She slipped unconscious.

"Don't worry, her heart rate is low but stable."

When they arrived, they threw open the doors and lowered her quickly. It surprised Darren to see such

"Sir - only family can see patients. Besides, she's sleeping right now. You'll need to wait."

"But - I'm her husband. She kept her last name after we married."

"Oh, well, you can wait in the room but visitation doesn't officially start for another hour."

The wait drew on uncomfortably. Darren tried watching the lobby television. All that played were early Sunday morning infomercials, evangelical churches, and TV-courts: all rubbish in his mind.

Did I do something to cause this? Did she relapse on my account or just relapsed the way I do? I shouldn't have snubbed her. She was my friend and I just abandoned her. If I hadn't of snubbed her, I would've picked up the phone. Of course, she might not have been able to speak anyways.

Her hand stirred then her eyes.

The tube through Sarah's nose made it difficult to speak.

"Darren," she rasped.

"Sarah."

Her eyes went out of focus, rotating sharply.

"I have so many regrets - you have no idea what I've done."

"It's alright."

"You don't understand. I'm a terrible person, Darren."

"Shh - shh. None of that."

"I've not clean of drugs. I've sold myself. I hate myself and I don't understand - I just don't. I'm a terrible person."

"You're telling this to an alcoholic who's been to a psychiatric ward. Two's company.

67

"Besides, I love you. If I'm allowed to be Raskolnikov, you may be Marmeledova."

She laid quietly in reflection before asking:

"How-"

"How can I love you?"

"Yes."

"It's easy - watch carefully."

Darren took his hands and rubber them together. He began blowing into them, getting them warm and then-

-stuck out his tongue and crossed his eyes, looking so absurd that Sarah couldn't help but laugh.

"You see, Sarah. With a smile like, you can't help but love."

He took her by the hand and suddenly the cold outside, out night, out right, now mattered less. It was still there, creeping at the fringes, but now it felt manageable.

Darren looked at her: blackened eyes, hair a mess, and a hospital gown the same pattern as the wallpaper, little blue and red dots on a white background.

Sarah thought:

I don't feel self-conscious anymore. I am free.

V.   Chemistry Rests: Michael's Story

In college, I started working at Glousters. It's one of those new-age grocery stores that try to cover up the fact they still have vomit, vegetables, and vodka behind the counters. That, "Hi, can I help you?" that's a pint of gin talking. The permanent smile is a woman trying to cope with losing her job, a decade before the company retirement plan's 401k matures. The tear behind the cook's eye, that's his way of hiding the betrayal of the girl in deli, just fired for lying about being late.

Fiona went to Canada Saturday night. She's not drinking age in the states. Anyways, she's late Sunday. Car problems, traffic, and homeless protesters: those're her excuses for calling six hours after her scheduled clock-in.

The cook, Chris is biting back tears, tossing stir-fry. He couldn't care less about her drinking or skipping work. He did care about their relationship.

Last night, she told him that they were now just friends and that she needed a break from their relationship: after months of dating, sleeping over if there wasn't a designated-driver, and holding hands. He was just a convenience, a condiment to put on life's troubles: something sweet to push away the sour of the day. So, he tearlessly cries, stir fry ladled into a sleek, black tray. He places it on the steel counter. A bit spills. He says, "So much for pleasing everyone."

Most everyone on night crew could call a place "home." Some called it Chris's corduroy couch -between barhopping-, Ralph's old embrace -as social security starts-, or even the overpass on highway 13.

Chris, our cook, and I are willing to call his '76 Gremlin home. We sit on the burnt orange hood. He sips a Guinness. I swig a Coke. If only we were 21 again.

Chris laughs, "What was I thinking?"

The bottle rises back as the last cars from our crew leave.

"Crazy - crazy world."

"I don't know: maybe, you weren't the crazy one."

"She's crazy, then?"

"If the glove fits..."

Those silences you hear when people tell an off-color joke - insert one of those here. Chris just stares at the drink. He's finished most of it.

"Just forget her. You don't need this: the flashbacks of what could have been. She's not worth it."

"Not worth it?"

"Trust me. She never was much else. She's like a buffet. Nice to look at; terrible after digestion."

I rest the bottle between my legs.

Everyone's sampled her anyways...

"What do I do now?"

"I don't know: get drunk?"

"C'mon, there' gotta be more?"

It's moments like these I blow. People want a gypsy, a prophet, not a high school graduate, junior college student working an entry-level summer job at a mid-range grocer. Here it goes: stop the drinking. Shave once in a while. Try not to slouch. Get a life outside of Glousters and video games.

The bottle drops.

A fist flies.

The world whizzes around me for once. Crimson light gels must be floating everywhere; that's all I'm seeing. Between a split lip and losing consciousness, I don't have time to consider how to react. My mind staggers like a young couple at twilight.

By the time I get home, the blood's dried to my white collared shirt. My boys are asleep in front of the television in the living room, the pale blue light flashing their silhouettes against the ceiling. Inside there's macaroni on some paper plates with bits of hot dog. Some spilt onto the floor.

I put a blanket over them as I strip my work clothes off. Another load of laundry. The twins, Aaron and Amy, are sprawled over each other, feet in faces and their little teeth exposed as they breath listlessly.

Jules, my wife, is asleep on the bed, passed out from graduate school. She's always so busy these days. You might think we're well off but we married at 17. We barely finished high school. She barely finished her degree while I worked here. We have twelve hundred a month in debts between loans, the apartment, and the two kids.

I never saw myself getting to this point by the age of twenty-six. I suppose we're pretty successful. We could've dropped out and I'd be working here indefinitely.

Gretchen works at Glouster's. She's a checker.

On a bad day, she'll put what little hair she has up: up with pencils, deli chopsticks, or Tootsie roll pops. The latter convinced me I was in love.

Almost.

I'd drift off as we talk; absorbed by the exaggerated hand movements she'd use to recall a particular memory. Her eyes would glow, like embers stoked in a fire.

Everyone else loved to joke "bruiser" to her as she walked past at work.

The story goes: a biker came in one night as Gretchen rocked listlessly between the checkout counters. This guy is wearing leather chaps, fingerless gloves, but his hair is too - perfect. It's partly the part to the right. Poser.

I wager he rides a ninja; a ninja to his telemarketing, assistant-to-the-regional-manager position. No true biker carries a blackberry. Not in the mind of a 26 year old.

Anyways, he asks Gretchen out. It was the first time I ever saw her get excited over a man.

I tell myself: *you're married.*

The twins' birthday is on Saturday. Eight years is a good age: they can play ball without it looking too uncool with Dad, they can clean up after themselves better. The only drawback is this is when interests develop in earnest. Soon Japanese animation replaces the Star Wars action figures; Harry Potter replaces the Redwall series.

I'm tasked with getting the cake and flowers from work. Jules is at a business and accounting conference in San Francisco. It put us back more (as in another semester I'll take off from school to focus on the task of getting people overpriced deli meats and pseudo-asian food) but she's getting closer to a degree.

I get off work late one night. We had this annual inventory before the holiday. Counting cans is easy; counting every can in a 40,000 square foot store is *taedium vitae* - suicide from the inside out.

Outside, the snows are falling like I haven't seen in ages. The I-5 corridor doesn't get too much snow, thanks to running along coastal, lowland inlets. So, here, in Burlington, we are covered.

There's that weird sensation when you've been inside without looking at a clock, only to emerge when the sun has set and the world is asleep. It's that feeling you get when you walk out of an evening showing of a movie to find the parking lot full and lights on.

My bicycle is around back, my sole transportation, from work, home. It's an old Schwinn, steel framed and tall, lanky tires.

Gretchen's at the far end of the lot with the biker.

"Please, just go."

"Not without a little something."

He leans in to kiss her and she pushes him away.

"Not today."

He gropes her now and there's this feeling curdling in my stomach.

This is where she gets the name bruiser.

She punches him directly in the face: the visceral meat tenderizer sound erupting and him stumbling back five or six feet. No labored breathing. She just shakes her wrist from the knuckle to bridge contact.

When he shakes off his own pain, he cocks a fist back.

It's then I interrupt.

"Get the fuck out of this lot or I'm calling the police."

He shudders, startled from tunnel vision. I yell again. "Get away from her, now."

He turns and leaves, getting on his Ninja and revving it full throttle. I go over to Gretchen and look at the blood across her knuckles. The skin is cracked and peeling a little.

"You alright?"

She looks up and shrugs it off.

"I handled it."

"I saw - gave him quite the bruiser."

The guy comes in some days later to the grocery store. His nose is covered in a butterfly bandage, bruised to his eye sockets, and his tail must be tucked between both legs.

I head toward the stairs but not before turning to Gretchen at the stand.

"Bruiser: on your back."

She looks over her shoulder and laughs approvingly, waving her fist in faux-angst.

"What's wrong? What's *wrong?!?!?*"

"Yes."

"I needed you to watch the kids on Saturday, Michael."

"Don't yell. It's an easy fix, I'll just call in sick."

"It's not that. You're always forgetting what I say. You never listen. Jesus, Michael, Mary and Joseph."

"I can change what days I work. You're being irrational. This is a very simple problem."

"Yes, but one we wouldn't be in if it weren't for you. It's always you."

"What's that supposed to mean?"

"I wouldn't have married you if you hadn't insisted after the pregnancy."

"I'm not selfish. I work my ass off to support the kids and you through school so we can both have work we enjoy."

"Oh - great. Hang that over my head, Mr. John Wayne. Am I meant to feel guilty? Forgive me, Michael, for I have sinned."

"Stop."

"Or what? You'll hold this over my head too?"

"Stop."

"Fuck you, Michael."

"Stop!"

I should've walked away five minutes ago. This discussion always comes up and I'm so used to losing. Now, I've not only lost but I'm losing it. I kick my foot deep into our wall, following all the way into it. Sheetrock dust covers my foot and there's blood where the wood cut through.

Jules just gasps at me, furious and surprised before storming off. All my timidity, my calm: it wore off today.

"What's wrong?"

"Oh, nothing. Just got into an argument with someone."

"Mind if I ask?"

"A little. I'm trying to forget it. I blew up and took out a wall."

"A wall? Jeez, Michael. You don't look like the wall taking type."

"I know, right? All of it because I'm working Saturday when I was told not to."

"That? That's all?"

"I know, it's simple but things get complicated."

"How does it complicate things? I'll take your shift if it's that big a deal."

"Well, it shouldn't be a deal at all but you'd do that?"

"Of course, for a friend. Yeah, I'd work at this dump another eight hours on my weekend."

She pauses as I finish my cigarette.

"One of my friends is having a party Sunday. I don't know many people there. Would you go with me?"

"Sure."

"Really?"

"Of course - you know, for a friend."

"Drink."

Gretchen hands me a tall glass of whiskey on rocks.

We sit. Every once in a while you meet that person you can just talk with: anything, everything. You get excited and animated, as if woken up from a lengthy sleep. It's startling; it startles.

"I remember reading Jack Kerouac just after the twins were born and -rather selfishly- wishing I were in his shoes. I'd look out the window and just want to hit some road. Drive to New York, drive to San Francisco: just drive until I finally reached that vanishing point on the horizon where the sky and the sea became one - then to New York to do it again."

"You beginning to get the bug, Michael?"

"I want to see more than just the end of the shift by the time I'm thirty."

"Yes - yes!"

I've never seen her so excited before. She's got this shine in her eye like she's a bit mad.

"My freshman year of college, I went on a road trip from Boston to Seattle, getting lost in Utah and winding up asking directions from this man playing guitar on his porch. His wife was pregnant but smiling, like the two of them had this secret and the whole world were the punch line. He kept playing but pointed me back in the direction to the main highway entrance. He just kept playing Friend of the Devil on the guitar and his wife offered some lemonade before I hit the road again. You would've loved the scene."

"I'll bet, bruiser."

"Stop! You've never going to stop calling me that, are you?"

"No - not on your life."

I stuck my tongue out at her and all of a sudden she's buried into my face and we're kissing. It's warm and firm. Our lips go back and forth before I open my eyes and she opens hers.

"Oh my god. I'm sorry."

She turns away, withdrawing her arms between her legs and cover her face with her left hand, obscuring it from me. I take it down.

"No, don't apologize. It's my fault."

There's this distinct pause, a chasm in the conversation that needed a bridge.

"I do like you but -"

"-but this is the last time we'll talk like this, right."

"I hope not but for now, yes."

I get up, surprised that the Bailey's is still laying on the laphroaig in a creamy velvet-brown layer. There's guilt on one hand and joy on the other. I finally found someone I can talk with again - someone that makes me not feel like a forty-year old man when I'm but mid-way through my twenties. I've also done the worst thing imaginable to my wife, mother of my children, and my confidant for these many years, despite how things are going now.

I stir my drink and the Bailey's and whiskey congeal. They wrap and intertwine but never really mix, they just rotate end over end and faster still until I give up and turn back to Gretchen, who is crying.

"I'm sorry but I can't. It's not you - it's me. I'm married."

She looks up heartbroken but not crying any more. I have reason to believe this isn't the first time she accidentally went after a married man.

It's my fault really. I never spoke about my wife at work, never wore a wedding ring for fear of losing it in the sink.

"That doesn't mean we can't dance."

Her look is puzzled and then excited again, she rubs her cheeks with the back of her thumbs.

We start dancing slow to Joy Division's "Disorder." Songs shuffle and wind and people come and go. We dance the whole night – no kissing, no staring in each other's eyes. That's that. Nothing else happens.

The party wound down around three in the morning. All the vehicles began backing out the driveway and lawn. There's a drunk passed out on a sofa in the front yard. The sound inside isn't quite dead and you can make out the faint sound of some steady, slow bass and synthesizer line.

"Michael."

"Yes?"

"I had fun tonight."

I flip my keys and consider what she says, all four words and their possibilities I must extinguish after tonight.

"I did too."

Jules is playing with the twins in the living room and I'm painting Connor's science project. Where other kids do volcanoes, we did this fossil bed with miniature skeletons waiting to be uncovered. There's a raptor, a stegosaurus, and a terrible lizard - the Tyrannosaurus.

The kids are laughing and Jules comes over, putting her head on mine.

"Nice bones - what you doing next?

I put down the brush.

"Just trying to figure out what I've done."

"Are you almost done?"

"Yeah."

Something is up and by "up" I mean down, metaphorically. Our sex life is fairly sedated but this - this is new. Five minutes, no climax for anyone and just silence afterwards.

Perfunctory is what comes to mind. It's by the numbers sex but without any of the color, just gray and quaint and tiring. It's bad sex when you feel tired from beginning to end.

I want to cry. I want to cry knowing she'll cry. I want to cry knowing things will never be the same, that I've crossed some line in the sand and everything changed in the space of inch. I went an inch, right? Unable to take it, I turn:

"There's something I need to tell you."

"What?" Jules asks, her back turned to me, half asleep.

"I - I kissed a co-worker of mine."

"... When?"

"After the party at work this week."

"Okay."

"Okay?"

"Okay - I cheated too."

"How far did it go?"

"I'm not answering this," she cuts me off.

"How far did it go?"

"We've been having sex for a few months now. There - you happy?"

"Did you enjoy it?"

"Sometimes. I don't see why you're putting yourself on a pedestal."

Her question catches me off guard as mine caught her.

"I'm not. I'm just trying to figure out how we got here in the first place. I mean, did I not love you enough?"

"No, Michael, not in the beginning. Not during the pregnancy. Not when the kids were little. Not when you started college."

"So why?"

She hunched her shoulders, sighing defeatedly as she laid down on the couch, hand on her head.

"Maybe it was the fight that set it off. Maybe I realized -I don't know- that you and I only got together because of the pregnancy. The whole nine years has revolved around prophylaxis not being used."

"I love the kids."

"Well, plenty of people love their kids and hate their spouse."

"You hate me?"

"No - yes. I don't know."

"Well, where do we go from here?"

"You're asking the wrong person. I've just been doing this because it's all I've known how to: love you, take care of the kids, and work at a crummy job. It's what I need to do right now."

"Why'd you kiss her then, if you love me?"

'I kissed back - why I kissed back? I shouldn't have."

"No one disagrees with you there."

"I felt lonely. I mean, we don't talk like we used to. Our interests have changed so much since high school. Back then you did theater and hated work, now you're pursuing a Master's in Business and Accounting. That's a leap.

"And me - I've wanted to travel, to see the world, to see something new."

"So, you kissed her because it was new."

"No, because she understood. I don't have many friends outside work. It's Chris, Darren, and Gretchen. That's it. I come home and it's you and the kids - who I love. It's just I've put myself into a box and she understood that."

"Would you do it again?"

"No - I hope not."

"Where does our marriage go from here?"

"I don't know. Aren't we meant to be angrier?"

"I think it was inevitable."

"You do?"

"Yes. That explains the calm. We haven't shared an interest since high school, save sex - and even that's gone stale as bread. We just should have spoken up earlier. I mean, we both saw it."

"Where does that leave us though - do we stay together for the kids?"

"You think two parents who don't love each other is a good example."

"Well, it's not entirely loveless."

"No, you're right."

She pauses after saying this.

"Maybe that's life - people intersecting at these strange points and going their own way. I mean, if our relationship isn't worth dying for, how can it be worth living for?"

"Do you love me then?"

"Yes," I say.

"Would you die for me?"

"Yes."

"But what if I wouldn't do the same for you?"

"Then we're over, right?"

"The kids deserve parents."

"I agree - but they deserve parents in love."

"So, this is it?"

"Yes."

"Jonas" – d.a. peters
Taken in Koliba near Bratislava, Slovakia

81

VI.   Jonas

On a cul-de-sac, toward the base of Squaw Peak along the Wasatch front, there's a hatchback pulling out from a drive-way. There were dozens in the Orem-Provo area: with technology firms, university professors, and financial businessmen that claimed these development communities. They were young models of American families: two small kids, a dog, a Roth IRA, and active in their communities.

Many were Mormon and took great pains to attend all their meetings. Their habits detailed in closely kept planners. You could see their lives mapped one hour at a time over day, over week, over month. These were journals of events, not the thoughts and minds that accompanied. From it -and their checkbooks- you could see a great deal.

See what people never planned on others seeing.

Jack Downey. Thirtieth birthday: the sixteenth of the month. Spent $200 on a hotel: Thursday. Wife's ultrasound results: fifteenth. Another $200 on personal services: same night. Wife, very pregnant in one photo; petite and athletic in an older one. Thirty dollars on "food" at the State Liquor store. Wife at Relief Society meeting: Thursday night. A receipt for condoms at Albertson's on University Parkway, same night.

Reading it, anyone would worry. They would see things, read things.

It wasn't what it seemed. The condoms were for a gift basket for newlywed friends in the congregation. Someone had to be realistic about their newfound habits.

The alcohol? It was for him. The bottle of Dom Perignon spilled during an attempt to loosen the cork, emptying all over the floor. The 200 dollars room service was a bargain bottle of Champagne. He noted that the cheaper bottle tasted better anyways, even if he would be drinking alone tonight.

He picked his wife up after the meeting. Julia'd slept most of the day and was surprisingly energetic. All the planning for the church's teenage girls. He wouldn't blame her if she fell asleep right now. With surprises, he usually caved and told her. He took too much joy in letting people know of his plans, as if everyone deserved to be in on them.

Tonight would be different, he promised. She'd had a rough month, the morning sickness lasting two weeks longer than expected. She felt bloated and fat. The gymnast's body she'd developed and competed with grew from 105 to 135 already. Her waist went from thirty to thirty five, which you couldn't see beneath the venous bulge. Maternity clothes didn't flatter. Elastic waistlines were something that reminded her of yoga, not a necessity in jeans. She felt worried too. Her plans of going back to work at the firm seemed hopeless. The recession had developed into depression for many banks. The investment firm didn't even have the same ownership after the banking shake-ups of 2008 and 2009.

She felt worried still after doing laundry earlier that day. She'd found some receipts in his jeans, which he normally emptied: condoms, alcohol, and a hotel. These made little sense and she hoped they were someone else's. She felt naïve for making such an excuse. Of course they weren't.

They were his. He'd signed for them no doubt, using his debit card.

Still, she smiled when she got in the car. This gave him hope.

The rain started up again and he turned the wipers on. The consistency of their rhythm made him blush a little at his plans. He was embarrassed. They were no longer kids, or awkward college students. He knew how to unbutton her brassiere, something that took less effort for him than his peers had suggested. They were no longer afraid to touch each other. They no longer feared that they'd be sent to hell. They were married and it was perfectly acceptable; no need to worry that their clergy and family would be ashamed of them.

She turned to him asking when they missed the exit. He smiled at her and told her not to worry.

The look she gave was the same as when he'd first asked her out to the Theatre. A playful, puzzled look when he asked her. They saw Gone with the Wind. He enjoyed it but protested at the audience's laughter after Rhett Butler forced Scarlett O'Hara into bed. She sat the next morning, eerily composed. The scene made him feel uneasy.

The face she made now was not the one she made after that scene. *Thank god.*

They pulled into the concierge pick-up. They'd never had something as grand as college students on honeymoon. The best he'd done for their nuptials was a Motel 8 as they both lived in the dormitories at the time, with a strict "No Boys in Girl's Rooms" policy. It was an odd rule for a university, especially considering they paid for the rooms, tuition - even the utilities.

He took her by the hand and gave the keys to the bell-hop, surprised by how smoothly things went. He'd never been graceful.

She turned her face to him, her dark brown hair falling over her eye.

"Wait, since when can we afford this?"

A question he hadn't planned on. He'd been carefully overwriting the cost of groceries and gas each week, hiding the money in the lines. He didn't want her to find out. Gas prices rose didn't they?

"Don't worry."

He grinned. It was that stupid grin of his that she admired. He looked so self-assured when he did but it always shone during uncertain times.

She knew pulling up that he'd rented a room but why? Why impress her now? She'd done nothing special for him as of late and this was a bit much for one of his surprises.

She didn't want to think it. She did anyways. What if this is an apology? Is this some way of him making up?

If so, for what?

Those were the type of thoughts she didn't want to have – but did.

They got into the brass elevator. The weight limit stated 600 kilograms and now she felt conscious of her own body again. Why must everything be measured?

He put his arms around her, hands clasped just beneath the bulge. Her friends hadn't put on as much weight so soon. She felt awkward, her balance displaced. She felt worse than the depictions in cartoons, as if she herself were a caricature, proportions stretched and warped and sagging.

She sighed and felt his warm breath on her neck as he whispered in her ear.

"You remember when we went to the movies on our second date?"

The image of him barefoot, walking the empty streets from the International Cinema screening on campus came. He'd been such an odd-ball, a goof and yet he could remain so endearing without seeming to try hard.

She whispered back in affirmation. Her cheeks started warming, though she was unsure if it were memories of him and her back now pressed against his body as they leant against the elevator wall or if it were the flashes in temperature she'd had this past month. She wished to get off her ankles.

The elevator chimed and the polished doors opened, swirling marble leading to room 518. He'd requested the room closest to the elevator. A good idea, he thought. Less walking on her feet. She'd been sore as a gymnast and was use to walking around this way but not tonight.

He picked her up, less sturdy than he supposed and they moved forward a bit faster.

At the door: a problem.

How to get the key out without setting her down? Of all the concerns and labors for this night: a key in his breast pocket now seem to unravel the moment.

He whispered about the key to her and she reached into his pocket, pulling it out. She couldn't have been the first woman to help a forgetful husband into a hotel room, could she?

A green light flashed and they were in.

He took several steps, wanting to make her feel light as if he planned on carrying her the whole night. The few times he used his gym membership seemed to pay off. He remembered having trouble picking her up when they married, back when he himself was thinner.

Looking at the iced champagne, the baby's breath on the blankets, and the red card: it finally settled on her. It had been another year. Two years since they'd married, just weeks after her graduation.

He'd been sent home early from an evangelical mission and decided to resume studies. He didn't want to wait for medical doctors to determine his eligibility to serve. He wanted life to keep moving at that fast tempo he'd discovered.

He claimed to have been released early just to meet her.

She took it in, a little breathless and feeling out of place. She'd forgotten the anniversary again.

He took her hand and sat on the edge of the bed.

They spoke for some time, laughing like they were kids again. She hadn't expected something like this. She forgot her weight. Forgot the swollen calves and ankles. Forgot the time she'd spent over the toilet this morning. Forgot how her bladder had caused her to leave the lecture she'd attended.

Then he kissed her and-

-her mind slipped and unburdened itself.

They hadn't been intimate for months now, mostly her decision, afraid he'd find her unattractive with stretch marks formed at her waist. She thought it absurd now. It wasn't like he hadn't tried a few times before she brushed him aside and rolled over in bed.

They started to undress and he laughed when her shirt caught on her belly.

Her face turned ash. He apologized, realizing the error. He now thought he seemed hasty and inconsiderate. *Laughing at my wife? Where have I come?*

She rose and turned toward him. They were naked now. She covered up, despite what they were about to do.

She'd always been conscious about her breasts. As a gymnast, she'd always been slender, build like a boy and rarely eating enough. Now that she had breasts, she felt awkward. They weren't small, firm little lumps. They sagged now, dropping oblong, not the pert circles seen in the grocery store. The ones you'd see before the black placard covered them up at the check-stand.

She held her belly too, feeling uneasy in front of him. How could he find her attractive right now? Of all the preferences she knew he had during sex, sagging breasts and stretch marks were not ones she was aware of. He preferred being on top too, which she now understood to be a technical impossibility, not without his weight acting as a vice on the child.

She laughed at the image of a baby with a cone shaped head, covering her mouth at her husband's bewildered expression.

He had never had performance issues. Now, he thought he might.

How often the both of them would laugh at their private thoughts, always wondering what went on in the other's mind?

"How are we going to do this?" he asked.

She smirked a little as they stacked and rolled, much like children's blocks. They finally agreed on the side. She wouldn't worry about him looking at her now misshapen chest or the stretch marks on her stomach. Her only concern was whether he could even reach at such an angle.

It went in and she felt a sigh of relief. For him, he barely felt it though it might prove to his advantage. He could focus without worrying about finishing too soon. He had tried not to masturbate since the pregnancy. She hated the idea but accepted it up till now. Better that he think of her than of the other women he knew.

The idea kind of revolted him though. A man so desperate, he couldn't wait nine months. He'd waited twenty-four years to lose his virginity. Now less than ¾ of a year was too much?

It was a strange position, working muscles he rarely used. The past year spent at a desk in a cubicle, reviewing schematics and drafts didn't help any. He found his wife more attractive pregnant than he did when they met. It was so counter-intuitive that he almost laughed.

He tried not to think of work but that's what he did every other time they were together. It helped last and he hoped she could enjoy moments like these. *Enjoy it, despite of moments like these.*

Soon ten minutes became twenty. Her breathing, even for her current state was rapid. She hadn't felt like this since early in their marriage. It was tense but good, like muscles wound at the end of the day, just barely beginning to unsettle. He kept moving, abdomen burning tight.

Then something unexpected, that both reached that point, without expectation. She whimpered a bit and he stopped breathing. Things went a little dead in the room. Waiting a moment, she rolled over.

They were facing each other, noses inches away from touching. Both smiled.

Her mind raced up again, weaving in ways he tried to keep up with sometimes. Labyrinthine, he called it.

She mouthed the words thank you, to which he did the same.

She looked away a second before turning back to him.

This was a question people asked each other but made no sense.

"Do you still love me?" she asked.

The phrasing worried him.

"Yes."

A pause.

"Do you *still* find me attractive?"

His turn.

"Of course."

"Why?"

"Why? Why I find you attractive?"

She nodded. "Now, I mean. Why now?"

He looked confused. She made her questioning face.

"I understand the question."

"So why?"

"Routine, I suppose."

"What was routine about tonight? Do you normally sleep with whales?"

"Well, if they'd look have as good as you, I'd harpoon them."

She turn on her back, laughing.

"Yes, Julia, I love you."

"Kettle" – d.a. peters
Taken St. Volodymyr's Cathedral in Kiev, Ukraine

VII.   Kettle

Damien couldn't sleep. Even with his eyes closed, he'd put in earphones with Elliott Smith crooning gently over guitar. He tried to silence the terminal: the rustled luggage, the coffee grinders at The Irish Pub, the chatter of Ukrainian Olympians returning from Beijing. None of it would drown. None of it would keep still.

Truthfully, he hadn't slept all week. It had been thirty days of irregular R.E.M: everything feeling like a stop motion video, his thoughts clouded and murky.

He sat up straight.

All these lives intersecting: strangers with name signs, taxi drivers hawking their experience, flight attendants in perfect stockings and impractical pumps – well, not the male ones anyways.

He'd been facing the wall and felt disoriented upon seeing midday.

A letter he carried weighed forty grams – pink accenting the seal. He'd held onto it a month now, unsure if he should open it. He suspected it would read like its twin, which an elderly Russian couple took May 9th down from a support on the Aurora Bridge in Seattle's Fremont district. They'd taken it just after making the call.

It was not stationary that kept him up. He'd seen it before, attached to a basket near the Lenin statue on Christmas 7th, before seeing it again the night the couple took it.

A jet engine roared, shaking him from that near sleep, that languor of the tired. The sleeplessness did not irritate him. His beard no longer irritated him. He'd never grown one before and didn't really choose to do so now. He simply let it.

He wore a dark coat and trousers but was not a business man. He'd never had need for a black suit, so it was more of a charcoal color, tiny streams of grey running through it upon closer inspection. The worsted wool did not irritate his neck.

Aside from the letter and his coat, he carried a small satchel. It contained a small carved chest with two roses braided together carefully. An old, baby blue piece of lace held them. He always bought them in threes but not today.

Almost noon. He should be leaving the airport now that daylight broke. He should be delivering the box to Daryna and Ostap. There were small trinkets in the box, tucked beneath the purple-burgundy velvet: an anklet, two mismatched earrings, and a tiny notebook with blank verse. They would appreciate it.

He could not read Cyrillic characters very well anyways. Nearly a year spent between Kiev and Seattle and he read – poorly at that. He could speak passably enough – even think in Ukrainian words when arguing or when making love. Yes, her parents would appreciate the note more.

He thought it appropriate to place both rings in the box. They were simple bands: white gold and very thin. They opted for no diamonds with a child on the way. Diamonds could wait until after the wedding.

He stopped. *That wouldn't be happening now – would it?* Maybe if he blinked hard enough, this'd all turn out to be a dream. All those sleepless nights, those times spent circling their flat, waiting for her. Time passed and yet the message machine still had two voices on it. Calling the number both gladdened and repulsed him. On one hand, things could return that way, right? Leave things as if she'd never left, so she could come back and be comfortable.

It repulsed him though. The concept of the message: leaving them static and immemorial. It felt sacrilegious even to his secular senses. That wasn't how things were but rather how he wished to be. To hear a voice he'd never expect to hear from again: a ghost in the machine. The pun could not cheer him in these thoughts.

She'd announced she'd be leaving rather nonchalantly and without warning. No one knew she'd rush off, headlong. Who could blame a man for thinking nothing of her going down to the water? It had been a beautiful night: perfect for swimming, perfect for taking off into the sunset, only to look back over the shoulder at how far she'd gone. She hadn't taken much: a fresh start in a new life – she'd convinced herself of this.

This is all a lie, he said, biting into a piece of chocolate in his pocket: cherry cordial in bourbon. It was quite strong and made him cough a little. They were her favorite but he suspected it owed more to her drinking habits than to the actual taste.

He blamed himself, looking over the woods surrounding the city. The sheer number of trees left him breathless. They really were forests. He'd seen Roma camped on the side of the freeway last night as the taxi drove. They were sitting around a bonfire with a mandolin, passing around a bottle. A year ago, the sight would've surprised him, like something out of the Quixote's La Mancha. The attitudes towards gypsies surprised him. They were treated much worse than migrant workers in the States: vehicles slowed down to yell at them, some arrested for no other reason than walking, and always spoken off like a contemptuous joke. He had thought attitudes towards Mexicans were harsh.

The way people treated each other or how they treated themselves. It was all absurd. It left him feeling indifferent, rather than more concerned. Hating people: be it gypsies or hating yourself, he was convinced, meant letting life's meaningless define you. If life were a cruel joke, it was cruelest of all to exclude others and exclude yourself from its struggles. If life were nothing but mere pursuit of a goal, why not pursue it headlong?

It seemed so simple in his head: a moment of clarity, like waking for the first time, conscious of everything as the light came through the blinds.

It felt too clear. Surely, Miroslavka and he spoke of this in their literature studies. They understood it on an intellectual level but why then did she do it? It made him think of others who had committed suicide in university: all smart and able to think so clearly at other times.

What had they concluded that he had not? What did they see that the curtain hid so well? What led them to give in to life's absurd meaninglessness?

Was it not enough to try to make the world a better place? Did people really need a reason to justify their existence?

Maybe there was no answer and maybe his head hurt at the prospect. He was over thinking again. The wheels started spinning – grinding at the possibilities. He understood the suicide to be wrong on an intellectual level but it didn't leave him satisfied. Indeed, the more bitterly pointless life felt, the more he wished to scream and curse her death. She had been his reason for recovering from depression in college.

He had attempted suicide since youth – not sad gestures but genuine attempts. An attempt at poisoning left him with bad but infrequent gas. A hanging had broken his nose – but not his neck.

It was her happiness that brought him out of his own discord. He had seen her sadly sitting in a library on campus. She came there each day, near the desk where he worked and sat writing in that tiny notebook. It had taken weeks for him to ask her what she wrote. She never gave a straight answer.

The moment her got her to smile and laugh, he knew he'd found a reason, something to shake his senses. It roused a part of his character he never knew existed. He grew outspoken: taking charge and caring less about life's annoyances.

He once walked barefoot in the bowling alley, rolling the smooth ball, and promptly turning. He didn't look back and didn't care much. Life was good. He had something to hold onto.

"How can you be so confident?" she asked.

He shrugged. It was not quite confidence but it was not the time to tell her that she was that reason.

"If I knew, you'd be the first to know."

"Oh - really?"

They hit it off and moved in together in less than three months. Neither did well with roommates, especially ones of the same sex.

Damien would cook dinner each night: creamed sauces over penne pasta, glazed pork, and fresh honey bread. He loved thick, hearty foods. Miroslavka felt at home with his menus.

She contributed the food itself, gardening on the roof of the condo with the other tenants. He joked that he'd make some man very happy someday. She would be drinking –say milk- and it would come running out her nose at times like this.

His sense of humor punctuated the end of every conversation.

And yet – he was not enough to save her from herself.

Not with all his John Wayne ideas – that'd he'd ride into her life and solve everything by himself.

He recalled the argument they'd had the week prior to the 9th: over whether to keep the child, over work, over those cursed rings:

"Damien, the kettle – can you not hear it? Take it off before it whistles too loud."

He stopped.

"But what about your parents? What would their reaction be?"

"My parents will be ashamed."

"They'll be shamed either way, Miroslavka."

"Yes, but this is more, I think.

"They do not know we have been together."

"What does that matter? We can be married before they know."

Her face took a blank expression.

He got on a knee and took out the small bands, holding them up to the candle.

Her face began to smile before she turned quickly. She faced away now, focus on cleaning a dish.

"Marriage?! You get me pregnant and think we must be married?"

"We've known each other for some time – I somehow think Ostap wouldn't be surprised. He's made it clear that it's your choice – your life."

"A rushed marriage is not a choice."

"It is an option though."

"No, there are not many options."

"There are other worries."

"I don't mean to be rude but I though having a baby would be good news – right?"

She turned away from him, bracing her weight against the kitchen sink, looking out over the water. She did not tell him that her loan had fallen through, that the bank demanded full payment. She had not told him that her Visa extension was rejected, that she had insufficient ties to the Ukraine and would have to leave the States. She did not tell him of how she paid for moving here in the first place, nor her lab results. It was her first comprehensive physical. She had grown up poor in the countryside but kept healthy in spite of it. She'd never had reason to visit a doctor when she arrived in Kiev, her immune system strong from those years on her father's farm.

She felt his heart and intentions were well placed – but placed on what little he knew and could really do. She would be sent back: penniless, with child, and expecting little more than nine years left to live.

"You have blue eyes," she said that night, turning to the window, watching the orange glow of the street light as the kettle boiled on the stove.

"Smoke and Oakum" - d.a. peters
taken near Iwo Jima

VIII. Selected Poems

<u>Turn the Record</u>

Sugarcane syrup dripping down
On her shoulders - these tight little curls
burnt red clay curdled
skin bronze with
rust specks spit polished
by a supermassive sun

Put on Elliott Smith
for a sad, sappy stripper
A drunkard who's just arrived sober
Runs over her toenails
As she walks off-stage
And out of the lime-jello gel-light
Her make-up is done like a theater student
might've done between scenes

Kalifornia

And Kali with her eighteen - no
her hundred arms
with a daughter
someone's daughter

Our time here just dissolves
Like the sand throughout the whole
As the darkness, just devours
The shadows with itself

Well, her daughter
an illusion
along with all that she creates:
like the hours
like diversion
like the love that people make

Choke on my words as the meaning won't come out
Of the basement

Go home, she says
Go home and eat your bread alone

A Portrait of Two Young Lovers

You still believe that we will rest?

It took the both of us.
Seattle took us.

"I'll come soon," she sighed.
"Not three, or five."

Then the rains
Turned the skies on themselves.
Cancers on a flesh sunset,
Before it bruised over:
Clearing,
Paving,
Cementing in September.

As I lay my head,
On the hotel room's pristine sheets,
Corners folded, triangles inward,
The half empty bottle of Sauvignon chortles.

She stood there, just then:
Bronze skin, full,
Elastic,
Textured, melted chocolate,
Breasts
Soft as ether, upright as clouds:
Better than I deserved!

And me,
all gaunt and pale,
a haunting on her days,
Ribs visible,
Wooded, hairy and blemished.

But gold tips copper
On a spool of cable
Moving beneath the streets.

The ruckus, the commotion,
A child's dream dying
into a man losing his mind.

There I loom,
emaciated,
over the bed,
a bed of crooked smiles,
half life,
and the smell of earthen blackberry.

Not love,
Not even close,
Not knowing,
but not stranger to the circumstance.

Something quiet, like a murmur,
or a foal, whinnied.
As her hair curls,
toes curl,
lips curl.

Nerves curled,
I'm curled,
Uneasy,
Stiff.

She convulses;
I never came.

Elliott Bay

Elliott Bay
Driving a wedge
From where money's made

The circus goes on from noon to morn,
wearing cheap paint,
red nose from a store.

Everyone's laughing,
it's a game you see,
of watching a man trip often,

Well, I'm heading southwest.
I'll pack my things
And fuck the excess.

Still

Hang my gray jacket upon the rack,
Undone MacGregor scarf,
Pull my fingertips through the gloves,
And pull my oak stool back.

Free Guinness, I grin,
Gaunt and grim,
At the IRA's messaging,

Put forty koruna,
On the bar,
Which leaves me
Two.

Cherry... Cherry Cola

A pixie
with a half a heartbeat
and a sore lip
pursing more than purses contain

Long eyes
wondering if the message
ever got there
ever went on the wireless

Folding laundry:
straps, shirts, knickers,
and crisping pins.

Rolling the wedge from her neck
As she puts away the clothes
And the wet bird prints
On the kitchen windowsill,

Go nowhere.

Skeptics Drink the Body or Our Lady of the Sorrows

The back pew,
the last pew,
The one closest to the door,
Dark wood,
Rose wood,
smooth finish to the floor,
Right wrongs,
Our wrongs,
And ripe, green eyes,
Pale skin,
Within a heartbeat's fist.

My suit's wrinkled, black cuffs uneven,
Her hair's a mess, St. Stephen's,
But we're trying our best to keep kneeling.

The echo from the 'thedral spire: slapping, pining, pinned
against the rectory.

All is silent, all is night, the stars are no longer in our
sights.

Winter Watch

It is black tea
with drops of honey
stuck to the bottom of my styrofoam cup
And I tilt and tongue it off my lips.

Heartbeats

As the heart beats-
beacons breaking
the horizon's silhouette
and the waves no longer
frequent your beat-
your breathing breakdown

I beat the steering wheel
with the sides of my hands
find rhythms and rhymes
that match the sound -
the sounding of your chest as fell
that night with breath

But those nightbeats-
those heartbeats in the sky
Just pulse, exsanguinations
till morning breaks.

The Doughboys Downpour

We're all tributaries,
Awash with needles and spawning fish,
And we're all running,
From a common source,
The spring near Mt. Sisyphus,
That always runs downstream,

And that pure, unsalted spring,
is something we have never seen,

Nor will,
As we empty into the jaded, salty sea.

Morning of the 28th

The drowning of the baby's rattle in an iron sea,
Memory pining through the windows of the pines,
Tastes without their sounds.

The twilight breeze of Juan de Fuca,
As pomegranate sun's pulse fades, and the twilight bleeds,
peels away to black, seeds take root in tongue.

About the Author

David Arthur Peters grew up in Washington State before attending Brigham Young University and majoring in English – a feat he never completed. He dropped out and joined the United States Marine Corps in 2006, serving in Okinawa, Japan and the American Embassy in Slovakia. An avid photographer, he now lives in Washington State again, pursuing a degree in "something or other."

www.ingramcontent.com/pod-product-compliance
Lightning Source LLC
Chambersburg PA
CBHW031850170626
46807CB00004B/1658